THE NEWSPAPER OF CLAREMONT STREET

THE NEWSPAPER OF CLAREMONT STREET

a novel by

E L I Z A B E T H   J O L L E Y

VIKING

VIKING
Viking Penguin Inc.
40 West 23rd Street,
New York, New York 10010, U.S.A.

First American Edition
Published in 1987

LIBRARY OF CONGRESS CATALOGING IN PUBLICATION DATA
Jolley, Elizabeth, 1923–
The newspaper of Claremont Street.
I. Title.
PR9619.3.J68N4   1987   823   87-40036
ISBN 0-670-80946-2

Printed in the United States of America by
Fairfield Graphics, Fairfield, Pennsylvania
Set in Times Roman

The poetry extracts appearing on the dedication page of this book are from 'Remembering', published in *Poems* by Ian Templeman, Freshwater Bay Press, and 'Town Edge', published in *Shabby Town Calendar* by Thomas Shapcott, University of Queensland Press.

Fremantle Arts Centre Press receives financial assistance from the Western Australian Arts Council, a statutory authority of the government of Western Australia.

The landscape of ridge, tree,
rock and valley, red brick, terracotta tile,
all leave fingertouch imprints
upon the memory,
slivers of images
beneath the skin.

Ian Templeman

For Leonard Jolley

there are no trees here no ghosts this is
the edge   tomorrows world . . .
. . .
the new timber grunts the owners change already
already . . .

Thomas Shapcott

THE NEWSPAPER OF CLAREMONT STREET

–1–

No one knew or cared where the Newspaper of Claremont Street went in her spare time.

Newspaper, or Weekly, as she was called by those who knew her, earned her living by cleaning other people's houses. Every day she was in some-one else's place cleaning. While she worked she sang,

> '. . . *the bells of hell go ting a ling a ling*
> *for you and not for me . . .*'

she liked hymns best and knew a great many.

'Well, and 'ow are we?', she called out, arriving with great noise, filling untidy kitchens with her presence, one kitchen after another, for she worked steadily all day, every day, one house after another.

She would start by throwing open the windows and, while the sink overflowed with boiling water, she would pull the stove to pieces. She knew everything about the people she cleaned for and she never missed anything that was going on.

'Who's getting married Weekly?', they asked her, and 'Who's moved into the corner house Weekly?' She told them everything they wanted to know, and when they asked more questions than she would answer, she said, 'If yo' know people is living, what else is there to know?' But she did know other things, deep hidden wishes for possessions and for money to get them; and there were wishes for those things which cannot be bought with money.

'I think that word should be clay. C.L.A.Y.', she leaned over old Mr Kingston's chair, 'let's see, what was that clue again?' She read it aloud,

> *Universal building material which does not endure for ever.*

You and yor intelleckshall crorsswords!' Mr Kingston smiled shyly down at the paper. CLAY, he pencilled in the letters. The word fitted. For some years now Weekly had taken part in one of his few remaining interests. On purpose, he did not finish the puzzle before her arrival. He took pleasure in the discovery that he shared with this uneducated woman a background of long Sunday afternoons which had been devoted to getting by heart passages from the Bible.

'Don't you remember,' Weekly said, 'let me see now,' she looked up at the ceiling, 'now let me see,' she muttered to herself, 'something like this', she said.

> *Remember that thou hast made me as the clay; and wilt bring me into dust again.*

They learned me that at Sunday School.'

'Ah yes!' Mr Kingston said in his kind old voice, 'Ah yes!

> *He remembereth His own who lie in the dust.*

'I can't say as I remember that part, Mr Kingston, but o' course it was a long time ago and they didn't learn us everything.'

'Chatham's girl's engaged at long larst', she reported to Mrs Kingston. 'Two rooms full of presents you should just see the jugs and glasses and the stainless steel cuttelry and talk about coffee tables and vawses!'

'Kingston's boy's ad 'orrible accident', she described the details to the Chathams. 'Lorst 'is job o' course but then that's because of what e's been taking, growing the stuff on a piece of clorth on top of the wardrobe. Whatever next! Missis Kingston said to me only larst time, "Whatever shall I do with this Weekly?" and there was this soup plate with the weeds growing, only they was all withered. "I think they must be bean shoots", she sez but I thought otherwise. "I'd water 'em," I told her, "looks as if they're on their larst garsp". Poor Missis Kingston my 'eart bleeds.'

Weekly sadly shook the table cloth over the carpet and carried out some dead roses carefully, as if to keep them for the next funeral in Claremont Street, which in her opinion, was sure to be soon. Seen from the back, the top of Mr Kingston's head dropping over the personal columns of an old *Sunday Sun*, gave an impression which supported Weekly's unspoken opinion.

When she went into the houses she saw what people were trying to do with their lives and she saw too what they did not try to do. Some things simply happened to them. The mess made by living did not bother her. People's efforts to clear up their mess were touching, their dead flowers drooping in stained, treasured vases and crumbs left in the bread tin made her shake her head and feel sad, not because she had to throw away the flowers and clean out the tin. It was the picking of the flowers in the first place and the buying of the bread and bringing it home to eat, they were the symbols of their efforts to live. Weekly made great efforts herself and was not unaware of the efforts of others. She noticed everything there was to notice about people and their houses; she could not help it.

She had worked for so many years in Claremont Street and had seen a great many people grow up and grow old. She could remember old Mr Kingston as a much younger man, someone to whom many people had turned for advice. Now he sat wrapped in red and yellow shawls knitted by his granddaughters. He smelled of a mixture of whisky and tobacco. Though members of the household paused briefly by his chair or put off going into his room for as long as possible, she realised that, unlike herself, he had relatives. His apparently useless life had been, and perhaps even now, was useful, even precious to someone. This striking fact about human life could never be ignored and, without ever mentioning it, Weekly was aware of it and knew its importance.

'I could not do without Thee Thou Saviour of the Lorst'

she sang at the Laceys while she washed the wrought iron trellis on the mezzanine terrace. 'You should 'ave seen the mess after the Venns' party', she called down to Mrs Lacey. 'Broken glass everywhere, blood on the stairs and a whole pile of half eaten pizzas in the laundry. Some people think they're having a good time! And you'll never believe this, I picked up a bed jacket, ever so pretty it was, to wash it and there was a yuman arm in it . . .' Mrs Lacey hurried to her walk-in wardrobe to change into something suitable for going out.

Weekly cleaned in all sorts of houses. Her body was hard like a board and withered with so much work. Her feet were so large and ugly with rheumatism, she seemed to have stopped looking like a woman.

On her way home from work, she went in the shop at the end of Claremont Street and sat there, taking her time, seeing who was there and watching what they bought. No one needed to read anything, the Newspaper of Claremont Street told them all stories and kept them up to date with the news. No one needed to bring a shopping list because Weekly knew what they needed to buy.

The boards on the floor of the shop were dark with repeated moppings with kerosene. Weekly sat on a broken chair propped against the counter. She sucked in her cheeks and peered unashamedly into the shopping baskets of the women who were hurriedly buying things at the last minute.

'Any pigs been eatin' babies lately Newspaper?', one of

4

the shop girls called out.

'What happened to that man who sawed orf all his fingers at the timber yard?', the other girl nudged the first one out of the way. Both girls had on new pink cardigans, both were good natured and plump. They ate biscuits and chocolate and scraps of ham and cheese all day.

'Yo'll not be needing flour', Weekly advised a woman.

'Why not then?'

'Yo' bought some yesterday', Weekly said. 'Now eggs yo' didn't get. Yo'll be needing eggs.'

'What about "No fingers" Newspaper?', someone asked.

'Well', Weekly looked all round, waiting for attention from the shop. 'He never got no compensation as he'd only been there half hour. Half hour and not a finger nor a thumb left on him. Both 'ands gorn and nothin' for it!' She let an impressive silence follow this appalling misfortune and, after a suitable time, she rose from her chair and went home.

She lived quite alone in a rented room covered in brown linoleum which she polished mercilessly every morning. Back at home she rummaged in the flyscreen cupboard where she kept her food, and taking out some bread and boiled vegetables, she sat reading and eating till she was rested. She was so thin and her neck so scraggy that, when she swallowed, you could see the food going down. But since there was no one there to tell her about it, it did not really matter.

There was very little furniture in the room and none of it belonged to her. All the clothes she had were given to her at the places where she worked. While it was still light, Weekly pulled her chair across to the narrow window of her room and sat bent over her mending. She darned everything she had; the needle was awkward in her fingers because the joints were enlarged with hard work and from an unnamed ailment in childhood. She put on patches with a herring-bone stitch. Sometimes she made the worn out materials of her skirts firmer with rows of herring-boning, one row neatly above the other, the brown thread glowing in these last rays of the sun which make all browns beautiful. Even the old linoleum could have a sudden richness at this time of the

5

evening. It was like the quick lighting up of a plain girl's face when she smiles because of some unexpected happiness. The corners of the room softened in this last sunlight and the herring-bone stitch satisfied Weekly with that pleasure which belongs to creative thrift. With the dusk came the end of her sewing for she was too mean to put on the light. She was tired and so was pleased when the darkness came.

'Mam! one of my titties is bigger than the other', she had called at dusk once.

'Oh never you mind!', her mother's weary voice had called from the wash-house. 'Just you wait a bit and some man'll knock 'em into size for you. Get off with you now to Granny Ackroyd's for the eggs. Hurry now!'

Weekly had never forgotten the dark lane alongside the pit-mounds, it was part of her early childhood which remained with her all her life; so was the strange old woman who kept fowls in a yard right up against the brick-kilns. The coal-mine was just behind.

'Hurry up with you', her mother's voice continued, 'the five o'clock bull's gone'. It was getting dark, the skeleton of the pit-shaft, where the wheels turned, was crazy and black on the sky left red by the setting sun. All day and all night they heard the throb and pant of the engines and the noise of the wheels turning, taking the cage of men down the shaft, and turning again bringing a cage of men up out of the mine.

Granny Ackroyd's yard was pit-dust and slag and sunflowers. The heads of the sunflowers were as big as Royal Worcester dinner plates and they grew like this out of this dust. Out of this nothing there also grew a very old pear tree. In spring Weekly stood pretending she was being married in the cascade of white blossom, but later, when the fruits came, they were small and hard and dry and had no taste at all.

'Yo' must never take a tree for granted', Granny Ackroyd said, 'same as yo' must never take a person for granted. People and trees is special. Always look at the tops of trees as you would look into people's hearts.' Weekly used to try to look at the top of the old pear tree especially if

Granny Ackroyd was about, but it was over thirty feet high, really as big as a house. Sometimes Weekly wished they had a yard and a tree; a pear tree of her own would be nice she thought.

'It's old, that tree,' Granny Ackroyd always said the same things, 'planted it when I was a young woman. Take some pears.' She offered the fruit as if she did not know how useless it was or, if she did know, refused to believe it.

Weekly forgot about her breasts almost as soon as she was aware of them. She was sent into service, and from then on hardly noticed her own body at all, being well covered with the uniform supplied by the Lady of the Big House. She was so busy having to learn and to do things for other people.

Later on when she saw young people on their way to the beach, she thought how lovely they looked. They were so well made and graceful. It seemed to her, that if she had ever looked like these girls, she had never had the chance, or the time, to either see herself as she was or to let other people see her.

The house where the Newspaper of Claremont Street had her rented room was large and had been built a long time ago for a big family. It had wide wooden verandahs all around it and, when she stepped on to the rough boards in the morning, she liked to think of the people who had built the house and the pleasure they must have had when they discovered that, at all times of the day, the verandah had some patches of sunshine, first in one place and then in another. Now the house was all divided up, a different life in every room and every life isolated from all the other lives. She paid no rent for her room because, before she left for work every day, she swept and washed out the passages and the toilet, and she swept all the verandahs.

When the first grey light of the dawn filled the narrow space of her tall window, Weekly woke up and saw the sky of the new day waiting for her. Every morning she woke with an aching back. Sometimes she ached all over and had to ease herself out of bed, groaning. This stiffness seemed to get worse every day, but fortunately it wore off after some

7

polishing and sweeping.

Some days it was so bad she thought she would not be able to get to work. While her body ached and was slow to see the reason for making haste to get up, her mind was alert. She knew she must go to work if she ever wanted to do the things she wanted most to do. And, with her eyes fixed on the changing sky, she planned which cupboards she would attack as soon as she stepped indoors at the Kingstons' and, before she put one foot out on to the smooth linoleum, she made a decision about the fate of the Chathams' shower curtain. She allowed herself the luxury of a few more moments, just a little time more, to think her favourite thoughts, and a glow of pleasure spread through her thin aching body. There was something she wanted to do more than anything else, and for this she needed money. For a long time she had been saving, putting money aside in little amounts till they became larger amounts. The growing sum danced before her, every morning growing a little more. For a few moments then, she thought about her money, calculating what she would be able to put in the bank this week. She was not very quick at arithmetic and it took a little time to do the addition.

She used the sky as a blackboard, and in her mind, wrote the figures on the clouds of the morning. The total sum came out somewhere half-way down her window. And then she rested on this total sum with the warm glow which had seemed to start somewhere in her chest, spreading and spreading over her body until, at last, she felt able to get off her bed.

Every morning it was the same and she groaned with every garment she put on. And, as she started to sweep, she was afraid she would not manage the work in the houses where she would be going. Slowly she swept, trying to force the ache out of her body.

'Hi Newspaper! Are you once weekly or twice weekly?', some boys hailed her from the street. She ignored them, forcing herself to sweep.

'Hi Newspaper!', they tried again. 'Did your nose get

8

born first and then the rest of you grow all round it?' Weekly sent the leaves and dust swirling off the edge of the boards.

'Nope!', she said. 'I chose me own nose.' And they went on their way because there was no answer they could give to this.

Years ago a policeman had called at the front door, frightening her mother. Together she and her mother had hidden under the table. They had seen the shadow of the helmet on the frosted glass. When no one opened the door, the officer had come to the back door and, letting himself in, had called out, 'Missis Morris, Missis Morris you can come out from under there.' As Weekly and her mother scrambled from under the edges of the table cloth he removed his helmet in front of the staring neighbours and stepped inside the small scullery.

'I'm here on duty Missis Morris,' he said, 'but you can boil up your kettle. I'll take a cup of tea at your table since I have taken this off.' Carefully he placed the helmet on the draining board and sat down.

The boys in the street reminded Weekly of other boys in other streets. The policeman had called that day, long ago, to warn her mother about Victor who, with other boys, was, as he put it, harassing the tram-drivers on the number seven route. Weekly tried to dismiss the memory. Her mother had been terrified.

There was something special about sweeping. While she swept, all the time while her broom was moving, sweeping and sweeping, her mind found a freedom that might be quite unknown in any other kind of work.

Weekly felt the fresh air of the morning touch her cheeks, it brought with the forgetfulness of sweeping, green meadows and willow trees along the flat, grassy banks of a river. This river was known as the Factory River.

'It's called ground baiting', Victor, hurrying on the grass, told her. Half her size, he knew everything. She was older and protected him, but he was the one who ordered her about. 'Ground baiting,' he said, 'you get the fish to come to your part of the stream, away from them. See?' All along the

9

river bank men were sitting huddled in the drizzle, hour after hour, hoping to catch fish. Together Weekly and her brother scattered meal on the slow - moving water. The other fishermen, some had their wives silently beside them, took possession of their stretches of the river in humped-up immovable shapes. Some of the wives had sour expressions.

In their enthusiasm Victor and Margie, as she was then, used up all their ground bait. They threw in all the ordinary bait and then their jam sandwiches and, without fish and without lunch, they set off hungry and wet and miserable for home. Victor consoled himself by throwing clods of grass and earth at his sister.

'Here! Take the bloody World! Here's another bloody World!' The muddy lumps flew towards her. Feeling sorry for this, she later liked to think that it was the reason, when they reached the main road, that he stepped hopefully into a dilapidated shop. As Weekly thought about the shop, she felt again some of the reverence she had had for her brother. This reverence was mixed with love, but more with shame when she recollected, all too often now, her betrayal of the one person in the world she had loved.

In the shop that day Victor, with his refined accent and his knowledge of flattering words and gestures and movements, describing the plight of himself and his dear sister, lost and far from home, moneyless too because of a cruel uncle, and on their way to their sick mother, had extracted from a shopkeeper, so hardened by lack of business that her eyes had turned to little sharp stones, two stale doughnuts from under a glass jar on the counter.

'Where's the fish then?', their mother was waiting for them at the end of the dingy street where they lived. Victor was ready for her with a neat little story about a poor old lady, with no home and no money, who had begged from them.

Quite soon after this life became more difficult for the Morrises. Mr Morris was kicked in the jaw by a dray horse and gangrene set in. After he died, Betsy, Weekly's elder sister, persuaded the family to emigrate. Betsy was in service with a family who were leaving for Australia, taking her with them.

Moving from one country to another had not suited Victor. Leaving his ambition for the Grammar School behind him, he was not able to adapt easily to the change of scenery and climate, and particularly to the people and the different attitudes he had to face. He seemed to feel the heat badly and he was too sensitive to the loneliness and the crude remarks showing lack of welcome to the new arrivals. Weekly realised much later, for she had not understood his behaviour then, his great disappointment, which he had never spoken about, at not going to the longed-for Grammar School where he had managed, by a mixture of intelligence and trickery, to gain a place.

Weekly and her mother were in service in a large house. House cleaning was the only work they knew. Between them, on swollen feet, they waited on Victor, cherishing him, because they knew no other way. And Victor, as he grew older, made his own life which they were obliged to hold in reverence because they did not understand it.

'But how has he harassed the tram-driver?', their mother's cry, so long ago, was without answer. Was it the fireworks, the jumping-jacks or those bombs he'd made, she wanted to know.

The police officer tried to soothe her, telling her it was none of these things. He reminded her that he had made a friendly visit. He promised not to put his helmet back on till he was clear of their place and the neighbours could see he had just stopped for tea. The harassment he said had been of the intellectual kind. But Weekly's mother had not been able to understand what that meant.

It was as if her mother's sigh persisted through the years, sadly and quietly, in the noise of the leaves fluttering in front of the broom. Weekly added her own sigh and then shook off the thoughts. It was such a long time ago now.

– 2 –

It was the time for Weekly to hurry out to her first house. In cast-off clothes of good quality — for, watching each other, no one in Claremont Street would have given her a garment which was worse than something someone else had given her — she was an unusual figure. All her clothes were well washed and well mended and completely out of date. She was tall and elderly and leaned forward when she walked. The sweeping had made her feel better.

Somehow the mornings had not changed since she was a girl. The big houses in those far-off days were all along the river. The water shone peacefully and the road curved round by the river. Through the trees it was possible to see the town on the far side of the wide expanse of water; clean and always looking as if asleep on the skyline. It was very different from the mean dirty streets they had come from. There, there had been blue brick yards and leaning fences. The tunnel-back houses were in long terraces, their entries echoing with boots and voices shouting.

Weekly, with her mother and Victor, lived in, as it was

called, in a large house on the river. The garden was bright with oleander and hibiscus and there were little orange and lemon trees in neat tubs bordering the swept paths. Weekly worked with her mother and Victor went to school. Betsy was far away in the wheatbelt, still with the same family.

The stillness of the river held a restrained power and the blue misty light made her mother feel rested. There was a great deal of work in the house, heavy china basins and pails to lift. There was ironing to do every day, starching and concentrating on little white frills, even their own uniforms and aprons took a lot of time and energy. Her mother was a strict teacher.

'Margie! you'um not to go in the master's study, there's big cigars in there and drinks and books with titles. Out in the yard with you and hang out the washing!'

No one protected Weekly these days. Everyone tried to get as much work from her as possible and she was expected to go into every room in the houses where she worked. But after all these years there was nothing, not even the *Seducer's Cook Book*, that could upset her.

She took no notice if there was a woman in bed, tranquil, with a Red Setter beside her, his head delicately on the pillow. Simply, she removed the remains of the breakfast tray from the hearthrug and later unfastened the door for the dog to go out into the garden. If she surprised people in their nakedness that was their affair. Clearly, in her opinion, showers should be taken before eight in the morning. If a bathroom was occupied she would say with a nod, sucking in her cheeks, clattering her pails and brushes, 'Excuse me gentlemen, I'm about to do the floors.'

She was used to people being in bath towels or in bed at all hours of the day. The intimate things which she could not help perceiving did not interest her much. If at the time of cleaning, various sexual or alcoholic activities of the householders were in the way, she simply cleaned round them. She was acquainted with, and quite unmoved by, their experiments with drugs and had tidied up on one occasion, quite calmly, after a murder. While she worked Weekly often

13

thought of her mother and all the extra hours of work she had done because she wanted to buy things for Victor. Later Victor had drained all Weekly's earnings till she had made her escape from him in a way she could not bear to think of now.

In those early days, when Weekly was a girl working with her mother, there was the freedom of the kitchens and the wash-house and the backyard and sometimes a vegetable garden and an orchard. It was like having quite a big house of your own, especially if the family went away on holiday, which was often the case.

Later there were changes and people did not keep servants, with the same sense of responsibility. Cleaning women came daily and, as household equipment improved, they came weekly instead of daily.

'Go through all the clothes Margie', her mother said, busily chipping flakes of the washing-soap into the boiler. 'Make sure there's no money in the pockets. Pound notes wash all right but there's no use in risking any.' The young men of the household were careless and Weekly's mother made a point of pinning any money she found in their clothes to the kitchen curtain.

'I found these, what are they?' Weekly handed two screwed-up pieces of paper to her mother who took them between two red wrinkled fingers. Her hands had been in the washing tub for hours.

'Where was they?', her mother demanded, holding the papers, still between two fingers, up to the light to see them clearly.

Her face was as red as her hands and arms. Her eyes seemed full of excited tears. The tears burst out of her eyes and rolled steadily down her cheeks.

'Go and brush out your hair and put on a clean frock', her mother said. 'We're goin' shopping.'

'But what about the washing?'

'We'll do it tomorrow. There's plenty of time. They're not coming home till the week after next.'

Weekly, or Margie as she was then, had never seen her mother so happy as she was that day choosing and buying

14

good-quality things for Victor. He had been given an invitation to join a Natural History camp and, because of not having the right clothes, he felt unable to go.

'I'll need binoculars too,' he said that night. 'All the others will have binoculars, you can't identify birds without them.' He stood, well-dressed and indignant, in the middle of the warm kitchen. Without binoculars the new clothes seemed useless.

The next day Victor was still disappointed. There were notes of anger and of tears in his voice as he told his mother,

'I can't go with these,' he said, 'these are only field glasses, and cheap ones at that, they're not the same thing at all. The others won't have any like these. They're not the real thing.'

Weekly's mother wept with the disgrace of having to go to prison for theft. She tried to explain to Weekly, it was not so much being accused of theft.

'I've thieved,' she said, 'there's no use at all pretending I haven't. It's bad enough me taking them two five pound notes which wasn't mine. It's a lot of money but not enough for what I needed to get and when I put the silver entrée dishes in pawn I fully meant to get them back before the family got home. But, as you know, they was home before I expected them and there's the washing not done and the ironing not done and the rooms not turned out as I was told to do. I've never thieved ever before in my life and I'm sorry.' She wept bitterly because she had not had the chance to explain. She couldn't bear, she said, to think of the family coming home to the terrible shock of the sideboard being empty of all those beautiful dishes.

'I never had the chance to explain to Missis Malley', she sobbed, and she plaited Weekly's hair into two tight plaits as if to make it keep neat for the twelve weeks they would be separated. 'Be a good girl at the Remand', she said, 'the time will soon go and you'll get used to it. You can get used to anything if you try. There's one good thing', she continued, 'there's one good thing come out of this and it's that gentleman who's taken a liking for Victor. That really is a blessing!'

Weekly's mother stopped crying and seemed happier as she thought of Victor having the chance to be a boarder at the school because the Headmaster felt he was an able scholar and had recommended him to the board of the school.

'That Headmaster really speaks nice,' Weekly's mother said. 'Have you noticed, Margie, how Victor's getting a really nice way of speaking now?'

At the end of the day Weekly was tired. She had been moderately fed in the houses where she worked. In spite of being watchful over each other's generosity the people in Claremont Street, in moments of conscious economy, remembered thrift when leaving something for Weekly's midday meal. Mostly she had hard ends of cold meat, an ancient soup and cake which had lost its glamour. In all houses an effort of maintained strength was expected from her.

She stopped in the shop on her way home and sat down near the counter where boxes of long licorice lay, and buns in glass jars stood on top of the cheap fashion magazines. She opened the fluttering book of lottery tickets with careful fingers and looked closely at all the numbers. Sucking in her cheeks, she mumbled the figures to herself, looking hastily all round the shop.

'Go on Newspaper! Buy one, only a dollar! You might win thirty thousand. Just think what you might win. Go on! choose a lucky ticket', Valerie called across the shop. 'Don't be shy! Just buy!'

'Yo' need to get cleaned up and swept up in here', Weekly told the girls sharply.

The book was tied to the counter with a string and so was the indelible pencil. A special hole had been made in the counter for these two strings to go through. She let the little book of paper fortune fall so that it was swinging to and fro. The girls knew she would never buy a ticket. It was just a joke to urge her.

But in a sense Weekly had bought a ticket without paying for one. She remembered the number she had chosen and, as soon as she was safely in her room, she wrote the number down on a card. And then days later when the lottery was drawn she carefully read through the numbers to see if she had picked a winning one. It was exciting like watching a race in which she was the only competitor. Her chosen numbers never came up lucky and so, with real pleasure, she wrote on the card next to the chosen number what she had saved by not buying a ticket. She had several cards all covered with small sums adding up to a total sum. As the lists of chosen unlucky numbers grew so did her totals and all this money of course was in her bank and not wasted on numbers which did not win.

So it was she saved in tiny amounts over the years, wearing cast-off clothes, working instead of paying rent, working morning, noon and night, spending very little on food, saving and saving for the one thing she wanted more than anything.

Of course there were other ways of getting money she reflected as she walked on the pavement in Claremont Street. Her skirt had eleven rows of herring-bone stitch worked in a heavy wool yarn, Mrs Chatham had unravelled a brown jumper to remake it and, losing interest later, she gave the tangle to Weekly who, patiently at dusk, finished rewinding the curly worms of wool. The skirt looked quite interesting, as if from a foreign country, the folds of it swung when she walked. There were other ways of getting money; she could have scalded herself at the Kingstons' or broken her leg at the Chathams' or, screaming, she could fall from a step ladder and injure her back at the Laceys'. There were plenty of homes where she could have had an accident and then claimed compensation. But Weekly had a horror of doctors and hospitals. An examination or several examinations would be necessary, and to be told to take her clothes off, as would be the case as soon as she entered the consulting room, was the last thing she ever wanted. In any case, she always thought of money in small amounts totalling up, it is true, into a large amount in the end.

'Two and two make four, four and four make eight', she often muttered to herself. Small coins and her old purse she understood. Compensation, with all its vastness and medical and legal ramifications, was beyond her comprehension. She loved her battered little savings books, one after the other. She cherished them, her babies, and she could understand the entries as they were made, every one, because she saw the pages with her own eyes, stamped with the correct date and signed.

Right after the beginning, or shortly after the beginning, she thought they had made a mistake in her book. Shyly she went all the way back up the Terrace to tell the girl in the bank quietly. She didn't want to get anyone into trouble for carelessness.

'I think you've made a mistake', she whispered through the bars gently pushing her book across.

'No Dear, that's your interest I've added on.'

'Interest?'

And the girl explained it to Weekly who listened with serious attention. On the way home she couldn't help laughing a bit, a sort of subdued private cackle, talking to herself, as she hurried across the little green park. It seemed that, as well as what she added by her hard work to help the total to grow for what she wanted, the money itself helped. Fancy money helping money, what an idea!

– 3 –

Claremont Street was one of the longest and oldest streets in the town. Several of the old houses had been demolished and new ones, in varying styles of opulence and architectural skill, had been built in their place. Two doctors lived in the street, two lawyers, several architects, some teachers and university people, and many others who busied themselves to great advantage in trade, even one family who had become millionaires in cooking fat. The variety in the street was enormous, both in people and in buildings. Opposite the shop a tall block of flats had been built, and in the immediate area were a few of the large old houses with corrugated-iron roofs and wooden verandahs in different stages of mellow decay. In the largest one Weekly had her room. All the old houses were waiting for the same fate, some day they too would be pulled down and the big old trees, Norfolk Island pines, Moreton Bay fig trees and the gigantic mulberries in the old gardens, would all be bulldozed and burnt and cleared away: New houses in Spanish or Mediterranean style would take their place, together with two-storey town-houses with white walls and red tiles, built in squares around car parks, and furnished with certain similarities of white and gold furniture, cream carpets, deep and woolly, pictures in gilded frames of the *Mona Lisa* and the *Laughing Cavalier* and little wax and plaster statuettes of Venus and Eros and the Kings and Queens of chess.

Two kinds of women went into the shop on the corner of Claremont Street; those who rode horses and played tennis and shared car loads of children to kindergarten and school, and an older kind in floral dresses and cardigans. They held coloured parasols over their faces, wrinkled and dried out years ago in childhoods spent in the goldfields; they dragged their shopping home in plastic folding bags bumping along on little squeaking wheels.

Years ago when the houses of Claremont Street had been built the people must have been puzzled over the spelling of the name of the street, at one end it was Claremont with an e, Claremonte, and at the other end there was no e. Both signs had been renewed from time to time but no real decision was ever made as to which was the correct spelling. These same people, years ago, had planted trees lovingly chosen for fruit and colour and size and scent. In every garden there was a lemon tree, a mulberry tree, a jacaranda, a kurrajong and a flame tree, as well as lantana, hibiscus, oleander and a species of giant cactus and huge bushes of the datura which seemed for ever in flower. The long white bells hung motionless filling the night with a fragrance which brought temporary oblivion from the cares of the day.

In spite of the piece-work demolition in the past fifteen years, some of these remained. The scarlet flowers of the cactus, together with the cat who had been there all that time, were reminders to Weekly of times gone by. She now spent her life entirely in Claremont Street, morning noon and night working with a thoroughness and a regularity which never failed, in one house and then another. No house was without a visit from her and her methods of cleaning at one time or another. Even in one of the flats where a European couple lived Weekly was employed from time to time.

There was a cat who was called Crazy by those who acknowledged her. She went from roof-top to balcony and back to roof-top. In some places food was thrown up to her as well as other things including old shoes and gramophone records, bits of wood and plastic containers—all of which were lodged along the gutters, higher than human hand could reach—when attempts had been made to move Crazy and her noisy companions to someone else's more distant roof.

Weekly was walking home after her usual rest in the shop. Her washed-out dress looked mauve and silky in the evening light. The sun had gone from the verandahs, except for the west side of the old house where she lived. Her room caught this last ray of the sun from the west. The herring-boning on the bottom few inches of her skirt looked attractive and expensive in the dusk; such are the tricks the changing sun can play. She was adding in her mind what she had earned that day to the sum which was slowly growing. Thinking of the money gave her rest and a kind of pleasure. In the evening she did not ache as she did in the morning. The breeze stirred her hair which was grey and ugly though no one ever said so; she kept it clean and that was all that mattered. As the breeze came she felt something brush against her legs and then Crazy walked in front of her so that she almost fell over her. She lifted her foot against the cat's body, only gently, to move her to one side but the cat persisted in walking to and fro from side to side, immediately where Weekly wanted to plant her own heavy feet, one after the other, on the pavement. Again she tried to move the cat aside.

'Yo'll break me bones if I fall!', Weekly muttered, trying to lift the cat with her old foot. But Crazy went on before Weekly, always in the way, and as Weekly opened the door of the old house Crazy went straight inside and, as Weekly unlocked her own door, before she could prevent it, the cat hurried into the room. This was strange behaviour for Crazy, who spent all her time, as far as Weekly knew, off the ground. Ever since parts of Claremont Street had been rebuilt

21

Crazy had moved up, as it were, to premises with more safety and a better view and therefore with more prestige.

Weekly ignored Crazy. She was used to being alone and she was used to rummaging in her flyscreen cupboard for her bread and boiled vegetables as soon as she came home. Next to the cupboard was a pile of newspapers and magazines. While she ate, she read the newspaper she had brought home from the Chathams' and which she would add to the pile afterwards.

Crazy, who was tabby, was old too, but not so old, as it turned out. She rummaged about the room in her own way. There were not many places for Crazy to search in, but she managed to give the impression that she was turning things over in the room, as well as in her mind. She jumped on the bed and gave herself a wash and then came down off the bed and over to Weekly and put a soft paw on Weekly's foot. Weekly noticed and shook her foot and the cat went back to the bed. Crazy repeated this several times so that, in the end, Weekly put down her newspaper and peered at her visitor. She got up from her chair and followed Crazy to the bed. 'Oh my Gawd. Not again!', she said, and sat down on the edge of the bed. The cat seemed to bulge and pant and, in between times, she put a paw on Weekly's hard thigh and Weekly stroked the soft fur gently. She wanted to finish reading certain advertisements in the paper before the daylight faded. But Crazy would not let her.

In a little while, in a tremulous bubble, a tiny black kitten was born. Crazy got up and turned round and round on the end of the bed swinging the kitten which was dangling, still attached to her, so that it smacked against the wall. The kitten began a thin crying and this brought on more panting. Soon seven tiny kittens were being cared for with the kind of single-minded unselfish devotion which Weekly had seen before and, on every occasion, had been more and more filled with admiration for this mother cat.

Some time later Weekly would have to find homes for the kittens. She chose their homes well.

'Mrs Lacey. See I've brought yor kiddies a little gift.'

'Oh Weekly you shouldn't have. Really you shouldn't.'

'Aw it's nuthin. Yerse that's right, in this basket.' Weekly lifted the noisy basket on to the table. Mrs Lacey was helpless.

The Lacey children had three cats by this time. All were gifts from Weekly. Gifts which it would not have been wise for Mrs Lacey to refuse. After all she would not want the whole of Claremont Street to know that she had not yet, in June, unwrapped the Christmas present her husband had given her. Foolishly while trying to add to Weekly's already overcrowded hours she had asked her to take down the packages from the top of a cupboard.

'I think it's a dinner service', she called back along the hall. She was all dressed for going out and did not want Weekly not to have enough to do. 'Wash it carefully!', she called, 'and put it away in the second sideboard, thanks!' She was in a dreadful hurry. She had so many dishes and glasses and plates that a few more really made no difference, even when chosen specially for her by her husband. Weekly knew she was capable of some uneasiness now and would not refuse the gift of another kitten. If it turned out that she was unable to give the kittens away she would be forced to dispose of them in the only way she knew.

Crazy, after attending to her babies, fell asleep in the middle of them. Weekly climbed into bed the best way she could with them all taking up so much room.

Before she fell asleep, she found herself thinking of Victor, Victor as a boy had loved cats. Long after he had given up playing, he would pause in his ambitious career to play with a cat. He had even had a cat once, Weekly remembered it suddenly; the only possession he had had for longer than a week. And then that too had been sacrificed as his other possessions had been and for the same reason.

Whenever she thought about Victor, which she did all too often nowadays, she realised that what had happened to him was bound to have happened. If only she had not played such a part in the whole thing herself. Trying to sleep, she remembered a splendid shop they used to visit together when they were children. It was in the expensive part of town and had a curved brass sill low down outside the bay window. Behind the bulging glass were trays and boxes and jars of sweets and chocolates. In European style, the sweets were wrapped separately in twists of sparkling foil and coloured transparent papers. The chocolates reposed, dark and rich, in beds of black and cream plush. Velvet chocolates, very handsome.

'They're hand made', Victor explained to Weekly, 'every one of them especially designed and made by hand.' They stood in the cold staring at the brightly lit world of sweets beyond their reach.

'They've got liqueur in them', Victor pointed to one selection.

'What's liquoor?'

'Liqueur silly! Spirits and stuff blended with eggs and things, curaçao – advocaat – benedictine – kirsch – kummel–crème de menthe.' He rolled the names off his pointed pink tongue. He pushed three pennies into her hand.

'Go in and buy some.'

'Aw, I dursn't.'

'Go on!'

'It's too posh.'

'No it isn't. I want some of that chocolate. Just go in and ask for that one.' He pressed his finger on the glass pointing at a chocolate whirl, a luxurious nest for an almond delicately frosted with something pink that glittered.

Three times, against her will, Weekly entered the shop and timidly offered her money, coming down in choice, every time, to smaller and more ordinary-looking sweets displayed on the glass-topped counter. The third time the owner of the shop came round the counter and opened the door for Weekly, overgrown and awkward as she was, to leave. Victor lay as if dead or in a fainting fit, his head in the gutter.

'Get him away from here', the owner of the shop growled at her and went back inside, the door bell swinging and clanging like an alarm.

'Oh my Gawd!', Weekly groaned aloud before closing her eyes, she tried to forget her brother, but in spite of herself she remembered things from time to time. And when one has had a long life there are a great many things to remember.

During the night for some reason Crazy moved all her kittens, one at a time, to some other corner in the room. Then, for some reason known only to herself, she brought one kitten back to the end of the bed and left it there so that Weekly was disturbed by its mewing which, for such a tiny creature, was a considerable noise and had a plaintive quality which made it quite impossible for Weekly to sleep properly. She dozed uneasily.

'Margarite Morris is the sun shining today?' Miss Jessop entered the classroom at the Remand Home. The passage boards and the stairs were reinforced with some kind of metal edging, it looked like lead. The girls were able to hear their teacher approaching for some time before she appeared. They were also able to hear each other; at times the noise of their boots on the metal was like machinery, out of order, in a factory.

Weekly, or Margarite as she was in those days, looked up at the clouds which filled the high window. Outside it was raining, the classroom was religious with the dark from the rain clouds.

'No Miss Jessop', she said after a pause.

'Margarite Morris you are quite wrong, you have forgotten all you learned the last time you were here.'

'Yes Miss Jessop.'

'Margarite Morris it is daylight outside, is it not, and the sun *is* shining up there behind the clouds.'

'Yes Miss Jessop.'

'Now copy down from the blackboard . . .'

There was a rustling and a scratching of nibs and the noise of pens in inkwells.

'Margarite Morris read out what I have written.'

'Yes Miss Jessop.'

*'The women are all keen-witted, clear-sighted
and practical in all affairs except love, do you
agree?'*

The word "love" sent a whispering sigh of laughter
through the girls. Miss Jessop rapped the blackboard with her
pointer.

'Before we proceed with our scripture we will add up
the marks of the arithmetic test. Every girl add up her own
marks, put down the total and then pass her paper to the girl
behind for a check over.'

The room was full of adding up; it seemed to get darker.
Weekly put her paper over her shoulder, she made her marks
78 and was quite pleased with herself but that hippo, Amelia,
who sat behind her, got them down to 68.

Miss Jessop recorded all the marks as the girls called
them out.

'Margarite Morris', she said, 'you don't seem to pay
attention. Can you remember anything of what we have been
reading?' Weekly stood up.

'Yerse Miss Jessop,

*'Shall the clay say to him that fashioneth it,
What makest thou?'*

'And exactly what do you understand by that
Margarite?'

'I don't know Miss Jessop', Weekly replied, 'it's in the
Bible and only God understands the Bible.'

'I see. And?'

'I like the Bible very much', Weekly said, 'I say a bit
before I go to sleep of a night.'

'Oh? And what parts do you say', Miss Jessop said. 'Can
you tell me one of the things you say?'

'Before Abraham was, I am.' Weekly looked at the floor.

'Indeed!', Miss Jessop said, 'and why do you like that?'
Weekly, keeping her head down, muttered, 'It reminds me
that this school and all the people in it are just nothing.'

Miss Jessop turned pale and twitched her dress.

'Margarite Morris you may sit down', she said.

26

Weekly missed her mother so much, and Victor. She hated life at the Remand. Miss Jessop seemed to find fault with her all the time. And then there were the dreadful washings in cold water down to the waist every morning and always the place smelled of greasy food cooking and, at table, the cutlery was greasy and smelled too. She longed for Victor's voice, even if he would be just calling her rude names. She thought about her mother and wondered how she was in the gaol, and kept worrying about Victor.

She ran away from the Remand. She hitched her brown overall in at the waist with a piece of blind cord to make it look more like a dress and she threw her apron away. Years later she regretted wasting the good calico, but this was only when she had embarked on her life of thrift where she wasted nothing.

She stood at the side of the gravel track, the heat was unendurable, it was something she had not had time to get used to then. Dry grasses trembled and the voices of the crows made her surroundings desolate. Her father had longed for the country always, all through his years stoking at the steam laundry he had talked of the country. He remembered wood-pigeons near a house where he worked when he was a boy, the gentle peaceful sound filled the morning. He talked of the fragrance of new-mown hay; but this country which he knew was very different from the place where Weekly was now.

Sometimes her father and mother argued about the country, their voices rose and then, in the little pause that followed, Weekly's father said, 'We'd have a pig license if we moved out.'

'What good's a pig license these days,' her mother replied, 'yo' couldn't make a living out of pigs these days, they're done all modern in big sheds now'.

'It's wrong', her father said. 'For pigs never to see the light of day', there was another pause. 'There's nothing so beautiful as the sun shining through a happy pig's ears.' And as there was no answer to this, the only sound in the kitchen was Aunt Heppie banging away with the iron.

27

Weekly longed then to hear the sound of their voices, as she stood at the side of the track hoping some cart would come along and give her a lift. She cried a bit for the old kitchen and for the childhood which had gone for ever.

'Yor Dad'll be here in a minute,' her mother often said, 'yo' better look out!' He was on shift in those days at the steam laundry and sometimes he made as if to take off his belt to give anyone who was around a taste of the strap. When Weekly heard his step in the entry she ran in and hid behind the mangle. Aunt Heppie too worked in the steam laundry and ironed at home. Every night she ironed white starched things, gophering with a special iron. The kitchen range was covered with different kinds of flat irons. Aunt Heppie held them up to the side of her face to see if the heat was right, sometimes she spat on one and her spit sizzled and flew off across the kitchen. Weekly longed to hear the steady bang bang of the iron as Aunt Heppie ironed, grim lipped, her face grey with fatigue and later it must have been pain, for she had cancer and sat on alone in the night by the small fire in the scullery poulticing herself with hot rags, and it seemed to Weekly she could hear Aunt Heppie wincing quietly to herself when everyone else in the world was fast asleep. It was soon after her death that her father received the fatal kick from the dray horse.

No amount of wishing could bring this childhood and its sense of comfort back, so Weekly dried her eyes and stood waiting hopefully. A long black hearse drawn by four horses came in a slow cloud of red dust. The manes and tails of the horses were tightly plaited with black braid, fine shudders rippled, one after the other, through their smooth well-cared-for sides as they tried to rid themselves of the flies. A second cart rumbled by following the hearse, a third cart stopped.

'Dear child come up beside me', an elderly woman dressed so flamboyantly that she seemed quite out of place at a funeral helped her into the cart. She peered closely as if she could hardly see.

'Poor dear child!' And as she drew Weekly to her she said, 'There! sit close, I'm all bones, but sit close or else you

28

might fall. The road is rough.'

The procession of carts with the black horses turned into a little, lonely cemetery of the kind that were scattered all over the place then. The old graves were almost hidden by wild oats. The cemetery was fringed with long-leaved peppermint and trailing eucalyptus. And the yellow-flowered acacias and other flowering trees made curtains between the graves. And among the headstones and crosses, all over the mounds, tiny four-o'clocks flowered.

A heap of fresh earth startled Weekly and beside the heap was a deep hole with pieces of wood laid across it. High above white clouds flocked without concern across a clear blue sky. Looking up it was as if she saw the sky and the freedom of it for the first time in her life.

'Poor dear child!', the old woman dressed in black and orange feathers guided her towards the grave, pressing her bony fingers into her shoulders. She had tried to get a lift to run away from the Remand and was at someone's funeral. Whatever could she do now?

'Your mother was a lovely person!', the old lady whispered and Weekly woke up howling aloud and was sick in the long dry grasses at the edge of the track. She had fallen asleep. No one had come by to give her a lift. It was only a dream and her mother was not dead, only in gaol. She ran all the way back to the Remand home and was inside the fence in time for the greasy food at tea time.

Now because she was sleeping badly these memories came back to her as vividly as if she was looking at an old photograph album and seeing pictures of the places and of the people.

Nothing had come along the track to take her anywhere.

— 4 —

Carefully Weekly moved her thin old body under the bed clothes. She did not want to smother the kitten. She would have to pull herself out of sleep, which had come too late, and get up and sweep and then go off to work, whether she wanted to or not. She must work and get paid. She wanted the money to add that day to the money she had worked for the day before. She rested a little while longer, lingering on the shining slopes of her money mountain, seeing all that the money, in its power, promised her.

The morning sky filling the narrow window was changing. A light, as if from pearls, came into the ugly room. Crazy was busy in a corner with the kittens, the first and largest one, still neglected, cried from the end of the bed. Stiffly Weekly got up from the bed and, taking the kitten in her large rough hands she hobbled across the linoleum on her bare heels and gently put the kitten with the rest of Crazy's family. But she might have saved herself the trouble for, while she sat taking up the space on the side of the bed trying to draw on her stockings, Crazy stood patiently with the kitten in her mouth waiting and waiting for Weekly to get up from the bed so that she could put the kitten back where she thought it ought to be.

Slowly Weekly attacked her linoleum with a rag soaked in kerosene and polish, she put the kittens on some newspaper and, after sweeping the verandahs and hosing out the toilet, she made her way to the Chathams' where she would be cleaning that morning.

Claremont Street was a very long street, lined on both sides with long-leaved peppermints, very old trees with gnarled and bulging trunks. In the very hot weather each tree made a little pool of shade and people, like Weekly who walked, hurried from one fragrant canopy to the next, the long leaves trembled and seemed to whisper with a faint rustling, even on days when there was no breeze. Some of these trees were being removed, one after the other, at the top end, as building alterations were taking place. Though the street was quite flat it had a top end and a bottom end in the minds of the people who lived there. The shop was at the bottom end and so were the remaining old houses including the large old house where Weekly lived. Opposite was the block of flats, it towered quite out of place and design. Its presence however had brought a great deal of custom to the shop and so, after the first shock of seeing the ugly building rise in its gaunt stages of construction, the people paid no attention to it being there.

Looking towards the so-called top end, it was possible to see beyond the suburb and the outer edge of the city to the range of hills, a scrub-covered, low escarpment, half hidden in a bluish haze in the mornings, making an horizon of mystery and promise. It was to this promise Weekly looked every morning as she walked, leaning forwards, her nose leading the way, to the place where she would be working.

Some boys in a passing car hailed her and, turning the car they drove up close to the kerb, slowly alongside her as she walked. Cheekily one of them opened the door and gave a whistle and made as if to draw her into the car as if she was a young girl hoping to be picked up.

Weekly turned sharply.

'Don't you know nothin' about age', she said. 'Can't yo' tell the difference?'

The boys shrank and the car drove on.

'How are you Weekly?' Mrs Chatham had a cup of tea ready for her.

'A ball o' dash terday', Weekly replied. 'How's yerself?' Mrs Chatham was never very well. She needed to lose weight. She had tummy troubles, 'My International problems'. She liked to joke about them, but at the same time seriously attended to her diet. She liked suggestions about diet. Weekly had pleased her last week by suggesting she sieve some prunes.

'Have you tried any of them little tins and jars, you know; baby spinidge and baby chicken dinner, all strained?'

'What a good idea Weekly!'

'Put yerself to bed straight after yer tea', Weekly leaned on the broom before attacking the laundry floor. 'When the babbies and the birds go to bed, tuck yerself in, get to bed really early for once. There's nothin' like a early bed. Early to bed early to rise makes a man healthy, wealthy and wise.'

Mrs Chatham listened carefully. Weekly found that quite middle-aged women liked the suggestion that they treat themselves like babies, even to the extent of bone and vegetable broth and being put to bed at seven o'clock as they had once put their own children to bed.

'Terrible fire they've had at the Bakery.' Weekly rested on the conversation. Though she knew of accidents and weddings, births and deaths and told the news from one house to another, she never spoke of the things that really mattered. About these things Weekly held her tongue. She noticed everything about people. She saw women spending lavishly on their clothes and holidays and on having their homes rebuilt and redecorated and refurnished; and she saw these women, at the same time, worrying, beyond measure, about the price of the meat they were cooking, she saw them almost count out the grains of coffee before making it, and she saw them wear themselves out trudging from one super-market to another to get eggs or cereals a few cents cheaper.

Weekly understood thrift for she cultivated thrift herself but what she was unable to grasp was the contradiction of thrift. It was stupid and small-minded to care about these few cents unless all cents were cared about.

There were other things too, intangible and touching in that they belonged to the mess made by living, but unlike bread crumbs and ashes and dirty finger marks and dust they could not be cleaned up or smoothed out like crumpled cushions and bedspreads. Weekly knew which wives didn't want their husbands to come home for lunch; she heard sons snarling at their mothers and ungrateful daughters banging bedroom doors. She heard the insincere voices and laughter in telephone conversations and she wondered how friends could be so treacherous to one another, so watchful over the successes and failure of each other's children. Though they had lots of people round them, and saw each other all the time, it was as if they were all really alone, and worse than this, though they rode horses, played golf, read books, looked at pottery and paintings, perhaps even made pots and pictures as well as dresses, they had not found out what they really wanted to do or to be. They all desperately wanted to do something. But what that something was remained to be discovered.

Weekly found great mental ease in the physical labour of scouring Chathams' bath. In the afternoon she would be going to the Kingstons and she was about to take a step in the direction she wanted to take in her life. She almost lost her breath over the bath as she thought about the event of the afternoon. She had waited some time, deciding to put off the suggestion she wanted to make till she felt the right moment had come. The excitement of acquisition was upon her. She had to make an effort not to dwell on it for too long. She did not want all her energy to disappear in her excitement, because she knew there was a heap of ironing waiting for her when the cleaning was done.

Victor, had he been able to know, would have approved

her method though he would never, for a moment, have understood or tolerated her thrift. Her method now, like his, involved understanding human nature. Quite early in his life Victor understood human needs and motives. He quickly knew how to excel at school. He saw what was needed and supplied it.

'Don't show me how to do the sum', he said to Weekly once, years ago, when slowly with her thoroughness she was explaining long division to him. His impatient clean fingers held his pencil poised. 'I don't want to know all that part, just give me the answer.'

He had hardly the patience to wait while his older sister covered the page with crooked figures, muttering to herself, counted on her fingers, crossed out and started again. As soon as she had arrived at the answer and was carefully ruling a double line under it he had grabbed it and rushed off to sell it to the highest bidder in the playground before the bell rang for morning prayers.

Later with his clients in expensive rooms Victor had employed methods which included a complete knowledge of human behaviour and reaction. Having expensive tastes himself he knew how to tempt and satisfy these in his clients. And this was how, in refined accents and comfortable chairs, he carried out his business. He discarded the unnecessary and kept his vision and his rapture on chance and on other people's money. His was a thrift of a different kind.

Weekly, keeping in touch with Victor, had no idea of what his business was and for what reasons people consulted him. That money was concerned she was certain, because it was the one thing Victor had shown a true affection for.

Sometimes, when he was ill, he suffered from a delicate chest, she visited him at his request, going timidly to the expensive apartment, taking with her, from the kitchens where she worked, delicacies she never touched herself. She watched him eat an avocado pear.

'I won't be here much longer', he told her, helping himself to the breast of a duck, orange glazed and succulent. 'I've got plans for better things.' Weekly looked shyly at the deep pile of the carpet and at the leather armchairs and the white and gold dining table which had light graceful chairs to match.

Weekly wondered how people could eat and like avocado pears and oysters. She often watched Victor swallow two dozen oysters as if nothing was happening to him at all. The first time, when she carefully gathered up the shells, he asked her what she was doing.

'To wash 'em o' course.'

'Wash them? Why in God's name!'

'To use next time.'

He had laughed so much he had to change the laugh into a groan, his chest hurt him.

Her mother had liked avocado pears. She said they were refined and elegant and she never sat down to eat one without a starched, white table-napkin across her lap. Sometimes she was offered one at the places where she worked, and at other times, she helped herself.

Perhaps it was a good thing her mother had died like she did. She simply refused to understand that motor traffic could not always stop for the pedestrian. No one saw or heard anything, least of all Weekly, who had been about to cross the road with her. It was a shock all the same and she had missed her mother terribly. Perhaps Victor understood something of this for he had come to visit her, looking uneasily around the room she had shared in those days with her mother. He must have been, Weekly realised later, counting up the value of the possessions because it was soon after that that he had wanted to sell the piano. But Weekly had never forgotten the visit, it was the only time he had ever come to see her.

It was hard work cleaning. Margarite – Morris – Weekly made three faces at herself in the Chathams' master bathroom mirrors. She made a fourth face for being Newspaper.

Victor, in spite of his ways with her, had never been false to her and he had never let her down as she had him. The pain of thinking about him was too much for her.

She went in to the Chathams' unmade beds. When

35

people open their doors for their houses to be cleaned, they open themselves. Every house has its own secret atmosphere which is exposed. Weekly, in the fragrance of the Chathams' clothes scattered by the unmade beds was grateful to be drawn intimately into the household, so that for the time being she need not think of Victor or his so-called friends. It was all such a long time ago now and so far away.

It was time to go on to the Kingstons. She could hardly wait to get there because of the thing that was on her mind. She tore off a piece of paper and scrawled a note to Mrs Chatham.

Next week the shower curting. M.M.

It was the promise of a treat, something to please Mrs Chatham, to make her feel her things were being well cared for. It was like the promise of something nice, she liked to give them treats. Weekly let herself out carefully by the side door and hurried as fast as she could to the Kingstons' place.

– 5 –

Everyone in Claremont Street paid Weekly's fares. She had put up the fares as prices went up. At first they did not know that she lived in the same street and so walked to work every morning and then in the afternoon walked to the next place and after that was quite able to walk home. From every household she now had, in addition to her pay, which was by the hour, and Weekly decided for herself how long certain houses took to clean and charged accordingly, ninety-five cents for fares. Where she lived and how she travelled to work was strictly her own business though they all found out in time, but by then the fare money was established and no one wanted to be the first to refuse to pay it and be the subject of the Newspaper of Claremont Street's indignation. It would be too conspicuous, and a great many more things would certainly be added. Indignation can spread and grow and include grievances, true and false, of a most personal kind, with the memories of the last fifteen years coming to life keenly and vividly with endless embellishments.

'Hi Newspaper. How ya' goin' ', Valerie the larger of the

two shop girls nudged Weekly as she went into the shop at the bottom of Claremont Street. 'What'll you have?'

'Oh, serve old Muttonhead first.' Weekly sat on the broken chair as if she would never get up again and watched the Doctor come in. She wondered what he had come down for. The shop was still an emporium, it belonged to a time which had gone by. Bolts of cloth were on a wide shelf next to cups and dishes and a glass case of faded haberdashery. The variety of goods enhanced Weekly's pastime of basket-watching. Sacks of wheat and laying pellets stood on the floor next to a modern biscuit stand. It was possible to buy an incinerator and a birthday card and a pair of stockings without moving an inch. You could buy kerosene and candles and icing-sugar and a box of chocolates all in the same breath, though chocolates were not a wise choice in the hot weather.

'Well what's going on in Claremont Street?', the Doctor said with a good-natured smile.

'Val get cigs for Missis Lucas's order.'

'I'm serving the Doctor', Valerie called back. Weekly sucked in her cheeks and peered at the little scribbled list he had.

'Yer 'fridge is full of eggs and butter', she said, 'you can crorss them orf, but yo'm out of toilet paper,' she added and sat back into her own thoughts ignoring a second, 'Well what's the news Weekly?'

She had news but at the moment it was private as it concerned herself. It had given the Kingstons a shock that afternoon when Weekly wanted to buy their old car. It was on their front verge between the box trees, crushing an oleander, with a cardboard notice, *4 SALE*, stuck on the windscreen. Weekly had watched over the car for some weeks.

'I'll take it orf yor 'ands', Weekly said as calmly as she could, hiding her excitement, and she began at once to clear the lunch table as if not noticing the confusion she had caused the Kingston family.

'You Weekly!', Mrs Kingston was unable to hide her

38

surprise. She was an English woman and used to not betraying herself, but her surprise was evident in every well controlled line of her face.

'Yers', Weekly paused at the sink, shrouded in steam. 'Yers, I could do with a vehicle.' Mrs Kingston smiled as she crumpled with kindness towards Weekly. 'Well I never!', she said.

A car was not what she was saving her money for but sooner or later she would need one. This one of the Kingstons seemed to be there for her just at the right time.

So of course Mrs Kingston promised to have the car thoroughly checked and various expensive repairs carried out which she had not intended to do. But her reputation in the street was worth a great deal more than selling Weekly a worthless car. Then came the discussion of the price. Weekly took no part in the talk.

'We plough the fields and scatter . . .'

she sang, noisily washing up, while the Kingstons talked on in their polished dining-room, their voices low in an uneasy mutter. Every now and then old Mr Kingston called out, 'What's going on?', but no one paid any attention to him. Weekly wanting to buy the old car was something they had not thought of.

'The good seed on the land . . .'

Of course they had to give the car to Weekly, for how could they, the Kingstons, though they always felt short of money, take her money away from her when they already had two other cars and two properties and a boat. And furthermore, Mr Kingston, in the position he was in, could hardly take back the charwoman's money.

It never occurred to them that every morning, before leaving for work, Weekly hoisted herself to the top of her money pile, carefully adding to the hoarded sum the extra she had earned the day before. They had no idea that Weekly's bank account, besides filling several bank books, filled her mind every morning. It was a daily vision, and took the form of an exquisite cone-shaped mountain made entirely of money, with a silver scree of coins on its steep sides. Every morning she pictured this shining heap, gilded on the rose-tinted sky of the dawn, before getting up. And when she was walking to work, her nose pointed to the horizon of promise; Weekly's money smelled sweet, it had the fragrance of roses and honeysuckle and fresh country air, and her thoughts of it caressed her face in the long fronds of the trailing peppermint as she walked from one tree to the next. But how could the Kingstons or anyone in Claremont Street know of Weekly's beautiful fragrant wealth.

No one could have any idea how much money Weekly had; it was no affair of theirs if Weekly chose to spend nothing, and to save for the thing she wanted more than anything else in the world. The car was a necessity, and it was with a quiet glow of relief that Weekly realised the Kingstons would not expect her to pay for it. She quite understood the delicacy of the whole situation and it was quite clear that no one else wanted it; it had been there almost seven weeks, sitting on the grass verge with Weekly's watchful eye on it twice, sometimes three times, a day. So she said nothing about it and, as she sat in the shop, she allowed the pleasure of possession to creep over her; she felt too tired to get up and go home.

'What you smiling at Newspaper? Got somethin' funny to tell us?' Valerie leaned comfortably on the counter. Just then Mr Torben from the flats came hurrying across Clare-mont Street into the shop.

'My wife Nastasya is ill', he bowed to Weekly and to the shop. He had white hair and very blue eyes and beautiful manners. 'Can you come tonight and help her. Please!' He bowed again.

Weekly did not clean in the flats, except occasionally for the Torbens. For some reason she was sorry for them, a pair of people who were quite out of place in the flats and even more out of place in Claremont Street.

Working, and being on the brink of the possession of the car, had made Weekly terribly tired. She was looking forward to getting home but had remained as if stuck with fatigue to the broken chair propped against the counter.

'Orl right', Weekly said. 'I'll come in about a hour.'

After Mr Torben had gone Weekly sighed. 'Now why did I say that', she muttered to no one in particular.

She walked home, her dress swinging because she was hurrying. The old material was beginning to look mauve and silky as the evening came on. She would have to pour some milk for Crazy, have her tea and then go across to the flats. She refreshed herself with thinking about the car, which would be ready quite soon.

There was nothing else for it. Weekly had not been able to find homes for all the kittens. While Crazy lapped greedily on the verandah, Weekly put the remaining kittens in a piece of cloth and carried them through to the backyard where she swiftly, without noise, drowned them in a bucket. She straightened up, pulled a few half-dry garments from the clothes-line and went indoors to eat her food, closing the door so that she was not able to hear Crazy's cries.

−6−

The small rooms in the flat where the Torbens lived were over-heated, and the plain brick walls were covered in pictures in oils and water colour, all painted by Nastasya Torben. Coloured wooden ornaments and hand-made jugs and bowls crowded the tops of the book-shelves. The bedroom opened off the living-room and Nastasya was sitting in the middle of the bed, which was so big it took up nearly all the space in the room.

'Veekly my Darlink!' Nastasya stretched out her arms.

'Mr Torben said yo' was ill', Weekly said. 'So I've come to clean up.'

'Torben say I am ill?', Nastasya cried. 'Ah! but now I am better. Since you come, Veekly, I am better!' Nastasya lowered her voice to a mysterious huskiness.

'But Veekly he is not Torben really, it is only that his name, our name,' she said proudly, 'is too hard for you stupid people to say so we change to easy TORBEN', she snapped her fingers. 'To us ziss name means nothing!'

Weekly forced her unwilling body towards the kitchen.

She had not started yet and already she was wishing she had not agreed to come.

'Not cleaning!', Nastasya cried. 'Do not clean. Tonight I am hongry, so hongry Veekly, cook for me tonight.'

'Oh my Gawd!' Weekly groaned to herself. Full of bread and vegetables herself, the thought of preparing food made her feel quite sick.

'See my wife's paintings', Torben pulled out some half-finished canvasses from behind the cupboard. 'From her paintings you can see what a sensitive delicate creature she is! When she was young you know, she had long legs like a colt and ran like the wind!'

Weekly paused with the potato-peeler in her hand and admired the paintings, a smile frozen on her tired face. She had seen them all before and heard the same things said so often. She would have to sieve boiled potatoes and make a smooth, thick soup just as they liked it; she would have to roast tiny chickens and scrape and boil young carrots and shred lettuce very finely for them. All this would take a long time. Her back ached over the sink and her weariness was made worse by their talk.

In this weariness the only thing which consoled her was the thought of the extra money for the evening work. She often did work in the evenings. There was hardly a dinner party in Claremont Street where Weekly was not in the kitchen crashing cutlery and dishes in the sink and commenting, 'Is that the Ridgeways you got in there? Thought I reckernized her larf. Can't stand the Ridgeways, not one of them, never could stand the Ridgeways', this last in such a loud voice that Mrs Chatham, trying to concentrate on her frozen peas, had to put the telephone directory down behind the kitchen door to stop it from opening all the time. Whatever would Weekly say next for all her guests to hear.

'I'll boil in this heat!' Weekly threw up the kitchen window, chilling the plates and vegetable dishes. Mrs Chatham always became so harassed when Weekly was behind the scenes at one of her dinner parties that she invariably forgot to serve either one of the vegetables or a sauce and had to show the guests that there had been peas. Here they were all dried up in this dish left in the oven. She produced the dish for all to see.

'Yo'll never carve with that knife.' Every hostess dreaded Weekly in the evenings and yet they could not manage without her. 'Let me sharpen it for you', and Weekly would march out past the table of well-dressed guests, and with a rasping, setting all teeth on edge, she sharpened the knife mercilessly on the laundry doorstep.

Dinner parties, weddings, funerals Weekly often worked back washing-up solidly for hours on end while people ate and drank and talked and laughed and wept. And while she worked she totted up in her head the extra money she was making and added it joyfully to her savings.

Here in the flat she had no chance to secretly visit her mountain resort of silver. Both Torben and Nastasya talked at her at once, telling her things about their lives and the hardships of being refugees crossing hostile frontiers in Europe with a few possessions hidden in their clothes, in terror for their lives. And then of their years in Palestine and Lebanon, places quite unknown to Weekly.

'My wife is, how you say, an aristocrat', Nastasya's husband said to Weekly. 'She is so exquisitely sensitive, if only you could read her poetry!' And then he and Nastasya spoke to each other in their own language complaining about the place where they now lived, insulting people who were kind to them, perhaps even insulting Weekly, but since she couldn't understand what they said it did not matter. Nastasya recited a long poem in this strange language and wept aloud. Mr Torben wept a little too, and then Nastasya suddenly leaped from the bed.

'Everyone is so stupid here, we have to change our name', she cried. 'But never mind! I am better now and the food smells so good. I will eat at the table', and with this announcement she drew the quilt about her and came in to the living-room.

'We must set extra place', she said and began rearranging the heavy silver, a few pieces saved from another world; they

44

looked out of place on the little card-table where the meal was to be served.

'You are our guest tonight!' Nastasya offered a treat and smiled her terrible smile in which her eyes took no part. She insisted on them sitting down and then serving them as if she were a butler, balancing the hot dishes and holding a spoon and fork in one trembling hand, her cigarette ash dropping gently into the food.

'Not too much, not too much', Torben begged his wife. Weekly, who had already eaten, looked at her plate with dismay.

'Eat what's set before you and no word said', Aunt Heppie's voice echoed somewhere inside her.

Half-way through the meal Torben leaned towards the unwilling guest.

'May we, Nastasya and I, call you by your first name?', he asked with gentle politeness. 'We should be so honoured!'

'O' course yo' can', Weekly was somewhat taken aback.

'The only trouble is', Mr Torben said, 'we have forgotten what your first name is. Can you tell us what is your first name please?'

Before Weekly was able to think which of her names she should offer, Nastasya jumped up from the table. 'We must have a dance', she cried, the quilt slipped off her leathery-brown shoulders. Quickly she pushed the chairs aside, clearing a little space in the over-crowded room. She wound up the gramophone.

'Torben will dance for us, a Russian dance! You will love it!' And then she switched off the light. In the darkness they all seemed to bump into each other.

'We must have firelight!', Nastasya's voice insisted.

'But we have no fire', from Torben.

'Oh my Gawd!' Weekly wondered where the light switch was.

Suddenly there was firelight. Nastasya crumpled some newspaper and lit it on the floor. She put on the record and shouted, 'Put on your tunic!' Torben obeyed and she shouted, 'Dance!' to Torben and he folded his arms across his

45

chest and began to dance to the music.

'Faster!', cried his wife as the music quickened, she threw some more paper on to the piece that was almost burned away. 'Oh the firelight is so lovely!' Grotesque shadows moved on the tiny square of ceiling and Torben danced a Russian dance, bending one knee and then the other and then both, squatting and leaping to the music.

'Bravo!' Nastasya was delighted, she smoked her cigarette and clapped her hands, and the flesh on her arms, flabby, quivered hopelessly.

Suddenly Nastasya stopped the music. 'My husband!', she screeched. 'He is ill! Veekly help me put him on the bed.' The fire had started to scorch the boards and the edge of the rug. Nastasya put the bed quilt on it and stamped it out. There was a smell of burning cloth and the room was full of smoke.

'It is only bronchitis', Torben said meekly. 'I have it all the time, it is my weakness, something left from years ago.' He tapped his thin chest; certainly he was very out of breath and his face was quite white. Sweat was in a dense pattern all over his forehead.

The two women, Weekly drawn in in spite of herself, helped Torben to bed. He seemed frail suddenly and very clean in his pyjamas.

'Fetch a Doctor pleeze Veekly', Nastasya asked.

'But it's after ten o'clock.' Weekly felt uneasy about going for a Doctor so late at night, especially as Mr Torben kept saying, 'It is not necessary to go for Doctor, I am ill all the time. I will be all right, certainly I will be all right.'

Between them she did not know what to do. She put the dishes in the sink; if only she had refused to come.

'Go at once!' Nastasya was severe. 'He might be dyink! Do you want my husband to die?', she wailed in a terrible voice. 'It is great privilege to fetch Doctor for my husband', she said.

And Weekly went out into the night. She knew from before there were no doctors near who could or would come to the Torbens'. Mostly they had quarrelled with all the doctors, including the two in Claremont Street. Before she left Nastasya pushed a scrap of paper into her hand, 'These peoples, doctors they call themselves, you cannot bring here,' it was a hastily scribbled list.

Weekly had to trudge the whole length of Claremont Street and then right to the top of the Terrace in the dark. She had heard that a new doctor had moved in above the fruit shop, someone unknown to the Torbens and who had no idea what was involved in going back with Weekly in the night to an unknown patient.

The doctor was already in bed but came down to answer the bell. She was rather young and, if she grudged coming out, she did not show it. She was sympathetic to the elderly woman who had obviously walked a long way on behalf of a sick man.

'What's wrong?', she asked as they set off together in the doctor's car.

'I'm not sure which of 'em's the worst', Weekly replied and could not be persuaded to say more.

Nastasya opened the door a crack and took a narrow look at Weekly and at the doctor.

'Her eye make-up is brown like a moth's wing,' she said, 'and her eyes look like insects underneath. Do not bring to my place again!', and she slammed the door on them.

Clearly this was a challenge and Weekly could see the doctor was determined to rise to it.

'I'll manage, you go home', the doctor said to the old woman. 'Have you far to go?'

'No, just acrorss the road.'

'Goodnight then.'

'Goodnight.' And Weekly left the young woman banging on the Torbens' door.

The next day Weekly, who felt exhausted in mind and body after the experience, she had disliked dragging the doctor out of bed, felt embarrassed too. The doctor had looked as if she thought Weekly was just as selfish and crazy as the Torbens.

Weekly knocked at the front door of the Torbens' flat

to get her money for the evening's work. Nastasya opened the door and listened while Weekly told what was owing to her.

'But Veekly', Nastasya said, 'remember I invited you for our dinner, remember you were our guest. And no guest comes the next day to be paid.'

And the Newspaper of Claremont Street had no reply to this.

–7–

Before Weekly got to the Laceys' she was tired. The mad wasted evening with no money to add to her mountain and Nastasya's remark to which Weekly had been unable to reply made her feel she could hardly step out on the pavement. She· was making an effort, a supreme effort, to get over the disappointment of not being paid. If the Torbens felt it was a privilege for her to work for them, peeling vegetables and cooking after a long day of work, and being battered by their conversation, Weekly did not share the feeling. But she was unable to put into words to herself the mixture of annoyance and indignation and hurt she felt.

Mrs Lacey was ready for Weekly.

'Take everything out of the children's rooms', she said as Weekly stepped into the kitchen and began pulling the stove to pieces.

'Move everything from under their beds and do out the cupboards, Weekly.' Mrs Lacey always wanted her children's rooms cleaned thoroughly. It was as if there was something in the lives of her children she did not know about and she was afraid of this unknown mysterious thing as if it was something evil. Every week Weekly cleared out the heaped-up innocence of the children, broken crayons, cut-out paper patterns, scraps of doll's clothes coming unstitched because the sewing had been done without knots to hold the cotton, and all sorts of things made with cardboard and beads and bits of string. She tidied the same boxes of stuffed dolls and animals and sorted the same shelves of picture books. There was nothing in the rooms except the stepping of children from one thing to another; and there was nothing in the remains of sticky sweets, stamps, sea shells, apple cores and other small hoarded things except the innocence of childish dirt and inconsequential untidiness.

'I can't think how they get their rooms in such a state', Mrs Lacey sighed. She was dressed for going to town.

'I'll go in there next thing', Weekly comforted her as she plunged the pieces of the stove into the sink, which was frothing over with hot water and detergent.

Like human bodies after surgery, the gas stoves in Claremont Street were never quite the same after being attacked by Weekly. Every week all the stoves deteriorated just a little more as she scoured off the grease and burnt coffee grounds and chipped blackened cheese and jam out of the ovens. It was the same with the shower curtains too. She never spared them. It gave all the housewives a kind of secure contentment. They liked, quite naturally, to feel the soothing comfort of having their things well cared for.

The shop at the end of Claremont Street did a brisk trade in shower curtains, parts for the stoves and other household articles. Weekly's harsh cleaning methods were very good for business.

'Margie I can't ever understand why you let Victor take your things.' As Weekly heard Mrs Lacey's car pull out of the drive and, with crashing gears, take off along Claremont Street, she relaxed into private thoughts and, as her arms gradually turned red to her thin elbows, memories came up in her mind.

'Margie I can't ever understand why you let Victor take

50

your things. You'll hardly have a thing to call your own, and you should never give him money.' Her mother had been quite angry and had shouted. 'He'll have us through the law courts and in the poor house before he's finished.'

'But you give him money', Weekly had muttered to her mother.

'That's my business', her mother had replied. 'And it's all the more reason why you shouldn't!' Her mother sighed, 'I don't know why he's like he is.' Weekly knew her mother would never look at the photograph of Victor when he was a little boy. She often looked at it herself. In the photograph he had round childish eyes, a little puffy underneath, and round cheeks and a sweet hopeful little mouth. Weekly loved the photograph. Sometimes she kissed it as she had done when she was a girl.

Her mother had a horror of poverty and when Weekly herself remembered what she had known of it she shivered with fear.

'Remember', her mother said, 'you must never give him your money. He'll take everything and he'll have you in the poor house.'

'I need the toilet', Weekly replied, still shivering. And her mother, sorry for frightening her, tried to comfort her. 'He'll have us both in the poor house before he's finished.'

On her fourteenth birthday Victor gave Weekly a present. She sometimes thought about it; it was a white, imitation-leather handbag with a broken chromium clasp and two handles.

She had thanked him.

'Aw! thank you Victor, but the clasp's broke.'

'You mean you've just broken it.' He was only a small boy but had a way of making her feel big and stupid. 'And mind your dirty hands, you're making black finger marks all over it', he said.

'Aw! I'm sorry', she'd said.

She remembered it as the only present he had ever given her. She had kept it always with a best hanky in it and never used it.

Weekly tried to think of her money mountain. Sometimes the thought of the silver cone brought a fresh breeze, laden with the scent of pine forests and cold clean air from the shining surface of a clear fast-flowing river. Things Weekly had never seen, but her money seemed to smell of them.

Thinking of her money comforted her and she wondered why she had loved her brother so much and why she had given him away to people who were so worthless and who had never done anything for him or for her.

She struggled back into the peace of the Laceys' house. After work she would walk by her car and see how it was. She looked forward to this. Her method of getting the car was, in a sense, a way of pleasing Victor. If only he could know, he would approve that she was getting it for nothing. But Weekly told herself severely that if Victor knew where she was or if she knew where he was, she would not have the car for more than half an hour and her thrift and careful saving over the last years would all disappear overnight.

As she passed the Kingston house she had a shock to see the car was no longer on the verge. It had been there so long it had become part of Claremont Street. Her first terrible thought was that Victor had come back, found out that the car was hers, and had taken it.

'Take a holt on yerself', she told herself. Her own hoarse voice, under the trees in Claremont Street, gave her a shock.

Of course the car was in the garage being fixed up for her. She hurried on home telling herself she'd be the death of herself, scaring herself the way she had.

On her door was a scribbled note.

Torben Very Ill Can you Come. Nastasya

Weekly sighed. She supposed she would have to go but she would eat her meal first.

Every time Torben was ill, and he was ill quite often, an earlier disease had damaged his lungs; every time he was ill he was a little worse than the time before. And every time he remained, after the illness, frailer than before. But every time

52

he was ill he seemed to get better with a tremendous determination and effort. He seemed to recover when all hope of his recovery had gone. It was as if he did this, time after time for Nastasya, as if he loved her so much he was determined to go on living so that she would not have to be alone.

Weekly squeezed a lot of little oranges with Nastasya and they poured the juice into a cordial bottle and went with it to the hospital. The two women, both elderly and, in their own different ways, strangely dressed, stood together at the bedside where Torben was propped up on several firm pillows. An oxygen cylinder hissed at his side and there was a mask on his face, the white gauze and the knowledge of illness altered his appearance so much that they might have been standing beside a strange man. A transfusion dripped tremulously.

'He vill recover Veekly', Nastasya whispered. 'He vill live for me, you will see!' Torben opened his eyes, they were as blue as always, and very tired. He looked at his wife a moment, tenderly, and then closed them.

'He vill sleep Veekly! and tomorrow all vill be quite better!' Nastasya was trembling, her hands were shaking but she gave a little laugh.

'The silly, silly nurses!' she said. 'See Veekly they have put his transfusion without first to take off his pyjama so they will have to cut off the sleeve to take off. Always they do this silly, silly thing!'

When Torben looked at Nastasya before he closed his eyes Weekly saw how he looked and understood something of his love and devotion. She felt in some way privileged to be present at the time of this tender look which lay for a moment on Nastasya. Weekly had loved Victor, she had been devoted to him in her own way. Had she been able to look at Victor again now, she would have looked at him as Torben had looked for the last time at Nastasya.

She tried not to think of Victor when she went to bed, at last, after her long day. She put Crazy out on the verandah and climbed into her bed. It was time to have the room to

53

herself. She enjoyed the privacy and quietness of her ugly room.

Sometimes when she was very tired Weekly's money stopped being a mountain and became a cradle. Instead of hoisting herself up on to the top of her shining money mountain she sank into a golden cradle; it had unlimited gentle musical depths and she lay resting, listening to her own lullaby of coins dropping softly as she fell asleep.

– 8 –

Weekly first went to look at the valley one Tuesday after
work. All the morning she was thinking about the long drive
and how she would be very late home to Nastasya. She had
thought it better not to say anything of it to her. Since
Torben's death Nastasya, unable to bear being alone, had
implored Weekly, 'Do not leave me Veekly,' she sobbed.

She beat her breast and tore her clothes and hair in her
grief after the funeral. Weekly did not know what to do.

'I cannot bear the noise of the cars and people goink
home at five o'clock and when it is half-past five and Torben
is not coming I really cannot bear! Veekly do not leave me all
alone in this flat.'

'I'll come in every day', Weekly promised, and for a long
time went in after work, forcing herself to do this.

'Hi Newspaper!', Valerie called out to her from the
shop. 'Where are you these days?' But Weekly hurried across
to the flats where always she found Nastasya, red-eyed from
weeping and her hair not brushed, sitting at the little table
surrounded by half-smoked cigarettes and Torben's photo-

graph, with his kind loving smile unchanged, in front of her.

'Photographs do not change Veekly even after a man is died', and Nastasya howled aloud. 'It is terrible alone in this flat, all the time I hear peoples but not anyone for me; I hear the lifts, and the wind cries like a woman in pain outside my window, and peoples pass my door laughing and talking. Hear the wind Veekly! Is like a woman moaning. All the time I am crying like the wind. These flats make a person more alone.' Nastasya sat all the time by herself and did not go out to fetch food and, though Weekly cleaned up, the flat became neglected and Nastasya was dirty and helpless. She seemed entirely without hope.

Unable to think of any other way of calming Nastasya, Weekly took her back to her own room one night and put her to bed there.

'It's just for one night mind!', she told Nastasya as she made a bed for herself on two uncomfortable chairs. 'Just for one night Narsty, to set you up, and tomorrow you'll be better. It's just for one night.'

A few days later they began fetching things over from the flat. First some bed-clothes and then pictures and then Nastasya's wicker-work trunk and various jugs and ornaments and books; and then her bed and all her treasures and Nastasya herself were settled and filling for ever Weekly's cherished privacy. Even Crazy had never achieved this. One night when the kittens were still very small, Weekly had put Crazy and her family out on the verandah. The next morning, when she opened her door, to her amazement Crazy was standing with a night-long patience, holding a kitten in her mouth waiting and waiting to come back into the room. All night long it must have seemed only a matter of waiting to take the kittens back where she wanted them. No one could wait like Crazy. Gently Weekly, with one foot, had lifted the cat to one side. She also understood patience.

The advertisements she read every night describing land for sale made her so excited she could hardly read them. As soon as she read one she became so restless she wanted to go off at once to have a look, but she had to contain herself in

56

patience till she had time to go. No one could wait like Crazy except Weekly. No one could wait for what they wanted as Weekly could and did. She was as patient as the earth when it came to waiting for the earth.

But even though Crazy had waited and waited she never was able to settle her family back into Weekly's room, but Nastasya, who had never waited for anything longer than it took her nurse to warm a cup of milk when she was a little girl, had a place in Weekly's room, and furthermore, to Weekly's dismay, filled it up with all her things, making it almost impossible to clean thoroughly every morning, as was Weekly's way.

'What time is it Weekly?'

'Diana Lacey I thought I learned yo' how to tell the time last week, shout me where's the 'ands are on the clock.' Diana Lacey was home with chicken-pox. Mrs Lacey, frightened of illness, made Weekly wash and iron all the curtains in case they were infected.

'Chicken-pox ain't in curtings', Weekly said, 'it's where there's children only and even then it goes orf in time.'

'Little hand's on the one, big hand's on the six.'

'Well an' wot time is that then?' Weekly rubbed the iron over the curtains, she had let them get too dry. She spread a dampened cloth over the material and steam hissed up on all sides of her.

'One o'clock', the little girl's thin, bored voice came through from the bedroom.

'Now y'oum guessin', try again!' Weekly spat on the iron.

'It's half-past one', she relented. She too was watching the time. She wanted to get off and go and look at the valley. She wondered which would be the shortest way to get to this place hidden behind the pastures and foothills along the South-west Highway. It was a strain thinking about the valley and talking gossip about the Chathams to Mrs Lacey and then playing at 'I spy' with Diana. It was a strain too thinking about the valley when she felt she had no right to go looking at land.

Perhaps this was because she had spent her childhood in a slatey backyard where nothing would grow except thin carrots and a few sun-flowers. And all round the place where they lived the slag-heaps smoked and smouldered and hot cinders often fell on the paths. The children gathered to play in a little thicket of stunted thorn bushes and elderberry trees. There were patches of coltsfoot and they picked the yellow flowers eagerly till none were left.

All land is somebody's land. For Weekly the thought of possessing land seemed more of an impertinence than a possibility.

Back home in the Black Country where it was all coal-mines, brick-kilns and iron-foundries her family had never owned a house or a garden. Weekly had nothing behind her, not even the place where she was born. It no longer existed.

The steam rose from her ironing.

'Iron bands on knickers', Miss Jessop at the Remand Home told the girls to write in their laundry notes.

'Please Miss Jessop my knickers haven't got iron bands on 'em.'

'Margarite Morris leave the room and stand outside the door!' No one could tell Weekly to stand outside a door now. Again she thought about the valley and how she would drive there straight after work. She had not had a great deal of practice driving yet.

The Chathams had paid for her driving lessons as it was unthinkable for them not to do something when it was known that the Kingstons had given the car to Weekly. That week she was heaped with presents of all sorts.

'What's the story today Newspaper?' Valerie leaned her bosom comfortably on the counter.

'Here's some lipsticks for yo' Val', Weekly sank on to the broken chair, tired as if she would never get up. 'They was given to me, Muttonhead's wife, yor sister ain't she?', Weekly teased. 'Yo' have them', she said. 'I never use 'em — they're yor colour ain't they?'

When she had learned to drive and had passed her test — this took great patience and it was not only her patience —

she tried to think of a place where she could take the car and drive to and fro on her own. The whole of the little township had been absorbed into a suburb of the city. The city, in the last few years, had become ringed with these suburbs. All of them had four-lane highways filled with traffic, high-rise dwellings filled with families, and there were modern shopping arcades full of clothes and shoes and food. They were decorated with designs in blue mosaic tiles. There were supermarkets and gift shops with big signs everywhere in wild coloured neon and American spelling. There was nowhere for Weekly to practise her driving, and then she remembered a lonely place behind the sand dunes where there was a concrete patch and a ramp, put there during the war.

It was to this place Weekly drove her car one morning as soon as it was light. It was the first day after getting her license. The municipality, in an endeavour to beautify the local beaches, had planted Norfolk pines along the edge of the dunes. Every tree was screened from the terrible winds by a carefully erected little fence. Weekly, intent on her clutch and gears, and concentrating on the position of the brake, had a riotous drive lasting five minutes, the concrete patch and ramp being very short, and in these five minutes, before anyone else was awake, undid the work of several men and countless working hours.

Fortunately she was unable to stop quickly enough and so gained the road, rather by chance than skill, before getting bogged in the sand.

Though she had driven quite a lot since then she still felt nervous before driving out to find the valley. Partly it was because she was tired. Her room was no longer the place of rest it had always been when she returned tired out after her long day of work. Nastasya sat waiting for her to prepare food and, as soon as Weekly stepped into her room, she began to talk.

'My Fazere, Veekly, had country Es-state with gardens and lawns and orchards, and every summer I ran wild there. You can have no idea of hot houses full with grapes and the fruit trees so laden, Veekly, the boughs had to be tied up with ropes. One winter, I remember, I had been ill and was there with my Nurse all alone except for the servants. Servants, Veekly, we had so many, two footmans behind every doors and a manservant behind every chair. Veekly I tell you . . .' Nastasya leaned forward always at this point, earnestly explaining to Weekly. 'I tell you Veekly, the washing of their white gloves alone employed five vimmin every veek—as I was tellink you I was there only once in winter, so cold, and my Nurse wrapped us both up warm in sheepes skins and we walked out in the night. Everthing is burnink I cried to my Nurse, but she say is all right, it is just the peasants keepink warm my Fazere's fruit trees to keep off the frost, and so it was, hundreds of fires glowing between the fruit trees, can you imagine Veekly, the orange-coloured flames leapink and the smoke hanging in the cold air, can you for a moment imagine . . .' Nastasya fell silent, brooding, she had forgotten the name of her beloved nurse. She sat for hours, often, trying to remember it.

'Pore old Narsty', Weekly said. 'You silly old crab, maybe yore old nurse never had a name!' Weekly was sorry for Nastasya. She had lost everything she had ever had. She had known such elegance and wealth. Torben had often, with interruptions from Nastasya – they always talked at once – described the clothes Nastasya's mother wore; the fine hand-embroidered gowns and shawls, and the diamonds that sparkled on the lovely white skin of her elegant neck. As she worked for them Weekly felt she had actually seen the comfort of this richness. It was as if she had handled the precious jewels in the Torbens' mean little flat, which was all they had to live in after the generations of family strength and wealth handed from fathers to sons and daughters. And as more sons and daughters were born, strength was added to strength in their inheritance and possession.

Through Torben's descriptions Weekly saw all this destroyed. She even felt she had been present when the great staircases were torn out and burned and the bear-skin rugs, tossed on to the bonfire, writhed in the flames as if they were still live bears. Nastasya had known all this, possessed it all once, but her background had crumbled, disappeared completely and she had lost everything in the subsequent flight.

'Pore old Narsty!' Weekly wanted to help her, but she was quite unable to understand that Nastasya, the product of her upbringing, was ill-equipped for the life she had before her and no amount of help from Weekly could make her overcome her self-centred arrogance.

'In summer my cousins were always there too and we stole the cherries, Veekly, you could not know these cherries, very pretty fruits, small and bitter in brandy, in beeg jars of brandy and my mother and my aunt, I always had to kiss their hands you know.' Nastasya carefully explained, 'My Mother and my Aunt was very severe to the servants. They thought, ha ha ha, the servants stole the cherries. Ha ha ha!'

'Naughty Narsty!', Weekly said, she was still reading and getting more and more excited over the descriptions of land and sheds and equipment. Now that Nastasya was in her room every night Weekly had to try hard not to be interrupted while she read about pastures and fences and water. An abundance of water, as written in the advertisements, seemed to Weekly to present moss-trimmed troughs one below the other, with paths of washed pebbles alongside. She seemed to see the clear water flowing over, from one deep trough to the next, all down the hillsides. The water was clean and bright and cold and there was plenty, so much that it overflowed and washed the sides of the troughs, cleaning the moss and cooling the feet of those who went there. When Weekly saw this water in her mind she could not remember whether she had once, as a child, been taken to such a place or whether she had only read about it in her reading book. She never saw water like this when she was out looking at the places advertised. More often the ground was damp and swampy, with only a doubtful promise of water in summer and far too much in winter. Sometimes there was a tank or a dam, nothing very big and certainly nothing so lovely as the troughs which overflowed in her mind.

Now that Weekly had her own car she was able to drive

out every Sunday to look at land, and her wish for some became even more intense. She did not want very much, just for a few acres to be her own land. She drove in the car to where the places described in the advertisements were. Sometimes she took Nastasya, and it was like taking a block of wood for a drive.

'Narsty,' Weekly said, 'turn yer 'ead and look at them trees'. When she was out she tried to ignore Nastasya, and she stared into green paddocks, fenced with round poles for horses, and scattered in the corners with flame tree flowers. Her eyes lingered on the deep grass, splashed white with lilies. She stopped to admire almond blossom painted on a blue sky and she longed for a little weatherboard house surrounded by glossy leaved trees, their neat darkness illuminated with oranges. She paused on the fringes of vineyards and saw fresh light-green leaves bursting on the gnarled, kneeling vines, and later the scent of the broad bean flowers made her even more restless.

And sometimes, when she went alone, she sat for hours in the scrub of a partly cleared area in the Bush and stared at the few remaining tall trees, wondering about their age, and at the surviving yellow tufts of Prickly Moses.

The Newspaper of Claremont Street knew everything and talked all the time in the places where she worked. She even knew how often the people changed their sheets and underwear. She could not help knowing things like that. It was not for nothing that she was called Newspaper or Weekly. But all the time she was talking she never complained about Nastasya and she never spoke about the land. Secretly she cared for Nastasya and secretly she read her advertisements and secretly she went off to look.

– 9 –

Weekly first went to the valley on the Tuesday afternoon after work.

'Tell me about Sophie Whiteman.' Diana Lacey was bored with her chicken-pox. Mrs Lacey was late home but Weekly made ready to leave, she did not want to be too late starting out. She paused in Diana's doorway.

'Well as I've already told you, she ate that much sweet stuff, chocolates and toffees,' Weekly rested on the door post, 'that she got a chocolate lining to her stomick and I'm sorry to say you can't live with a chocolate lining in yor stomick.'

'Did she die?'

'I'm afraid she did and so would any of us!', Weekly said and she left Diana contemplating the enviable death of this girl Sophie Whiteman.

Weekly knew she had to cross the Medulla brook and turn left at the twenty-nine-mile peg. She found the valley all right. After the turn-off the road bends and climbs and then there it is, lush pasture on either side of the road with cattle grazing, straying towards a three-cornered dam. Each hour of the day is different because of the ever changing position of the sun and no day is exactly as the day which has gone before, and Weekly never saw the valley again in quite the same enchanted light of the afternoon as she did on the first day. And, on that first day there was a newly born calf which was struggling to get up on its little legs.

She saw the weatherboard house. The yard and the paddock were taken over by castor oil plants and the fences and sheds were grey and crazy with old age but Weekly trembled with the delight of being able to find out about it.

> *'Rock of ages cleft for me*
> *Let me to thy bosom fly'*

she sang to herself in her strange hoarse voice as she strode up the track to the house.

> *'While the gathering waters roll*
> *While the tempests still are nigh . . .'*

Singing gave her strength. She knocked.

'Excuse me, but can yo' tell me what part of the land's for sale?', her voice shook.

The young woman, the tenant's wife, came out.

'It's all for sale', she said. They walked side by side.

'All up there', the young woman pointed to the hillside where it was steep and covered with dead trees and rocks and pig-sties made from old railway-sleepers and blistered corrugated iron. Beyond was the light and shade of the sun shining through the jarrah trees.

'And down there', she flung her plump arm, mottled from being too near the stove, towards the meadow which lay smiling below.

'There's a few orange trees all neglected', she explained. 'That in the middle is an apricot. You should have seen the boxes of fruit from that one tree. That over there in the swamp is a pear tree. And where you see them white lilies, that's where there's an old well. Seventeen acres this side.'

They walked back towards the house.

'The pasture's leased just now', the young woman explained. 'But it's all for sale, thirty acres and there's another eighteen, uncleared in the scrub.'

Weekly wanted to look inside the shabby house but she felt it would be an intrusion. This was a new feeling for her. Her presence and personality had a value all their own and she knew that, when she stepped into a house, she had a place there and was welcome. She knew her very presence seemed to tidy and clean a house even before she had taken the broom or picked up the pail and scrubbing brush. The feeling of intruding upon this house, which was really meant to be looked at, was something unexpected, and so Weekly did not ask to see it. She would have liked to stay looking at the valley, but dressed in her faded working clothes, she was afraid that the young woman would not believe she really wanted to buy some of it. She drove home in a golden tranquillity, dreaming of her land bulging with plump apricots, fragrant with these glowing golden fruits, and embroidered with pear blossom, the flowers already cascading about her in white showers. Her crooked feet were wet from the long grass and yellow-daisied cape weed of the damp meadow.

The road turned and dropped and below was the great plain. The neat ribs of the vineyards chased each other towards the vague outlines of the city. Beyond was a thin curving line, shining like the gilded rim of a china saucer. It was the sea, brimming, joining the earth to the sky.

Nastasya had not noticed at all that Weekly was so late home. She was stripped naked sponging her brownish leathery body with cold water.

'You should take cold bath Veekly', she said, her withered breasts hung over the enamel basin. She looked pathetic in the ugly room.

'Help me Veekly!', she held out the face-cloth dripping with water. 'I cannot wash my neck.'

'Just you mind my floor!', Weekly muttered. 'Just you look at all that mess you've made!'

'Veekly help me to wash myself, rub my back so.

Veekly help me, I am not stronk any more.'

Weekly's cheeks were flushed from the fresh air of the valley and she was tired and hungry. Straight away she busied herself at the flyscreen cupboard searching for her bread and boiled carrots.

'Oh oh!', Nastasya wailed. 'My legs is all covered in hairs.'

'Well be glad they're not all over yor face!'

'Is all right for you Veekly your flesh just fit your bones so nice but I am getting old!' Nastasya began to cry, the water still dripping on the floor. 'I am getting all old and wrinkled, look at my flabby thighs. Oh!'

Weekly was getting older too, every day she learned a great deal about getting older. And not only the aching, it was the speed with which time passed. The days went by so quickly it was like turning over the pages of a book without reading any of them. If she did not make haste and buy her land it would soon be too late to buy any. She tried to keep her restlessness from coming back as she thought of the valley; and she tried to ignore Nastasya. It was a pity Nastasya no longer painted, it would have been something for her to do. Only destruction was in her mind now, and in her fingers, for she seemed deeply depressed, so that everything around her became lifeless. Even when Weekly polished her linoleum or stitched another row of herring-bone it seemed to be a waste of time, so much did Nastasya give off an atmosphere of waste and uselessness. Weekly wished every day that there might be some opportunity to get rid of her unwanted guest. She couldn't bring herself to turn her out, for the hospital was the only place where she could go.

'You ought to be pleased and grateful you are so much loved', Nastasya reproached Weekly. 'Only a few peoples is ever really loved,' she added.

'Get dressed!' Weekly sat with her back to Nastasya and ate her food.

'When I was young,' Nastasya talked on and on, 'I had long legs like a colt and I ran wild . . .'

'Did you now!'

66

'I loved horses and dogs, I loved all animals. Animals you know Veekly is better than peoples. Except for Torben all animals is better than peoples. On my marriage night Veekly, Torben he beat me! Torben I say why you beat me so thump! thump! He was not Torben really, his name is too difficult for you stupid people to say so he change to Torben. Torben I say why you beat so stop! And he wake up then. Why my Dear he say I was sleepink what is wronk Darlink? You beat me so thump thump I say and he say oh I dream I have dream I am Hussar back with Cossack and I beat my lazy servant so thump thump get up you lazy good-for-nothing thump bring me my tea thump light the samovar—my Dear so sorry but I was sleepink.'

'Did you now!' Weekly chewed her food. While Nastasya talked, distaste spread from Nastasya to the food. Weekly scratched her arms. She was forced to stop thinking about the valley. Whatever could she do with Nastasya. She had become an obstacle, a kind of wall which Weekly would have to climb over every day before she could do anything. As well as having to care for her and prepare her food, these things took time and Weekly had very little time—there was the burden of this endless talking, just when she wanted to be quietly with her own thoughts.

'Veekly I really have no strength. I may faint!'

'I'll be here Narsty if yo' faint.' Weekly sat on with her back to the leathery nakedness and the dripping sponge. She did not want to look at Nastasya. 'Just you hurry up and get washed and dressed. You won't faint, not from being clean, any-road.'

Nastasya said something angrily in her own language and Weekly went on with her meal, which she hardly wanted now. She could hear Nastasya grumbling and fidgetting about but refused to turn round. Usually she had to force Nastasya to wipe her face with a damp cloth and she had often struggled to drag a comb through her neglected hair. She felt threatened by this change in Nastasya's behaviour.

'The Arabs you know, Veekly . . .' Nastasya's voice went on as before. 'The Arabs, Veekly, leave their old people and their sick peoples to die—they leave them outside their houses, in ditches or by the side of the road. They have to, there is no other way. It is bad but it is the only way for them. I like Arabs very much, Veekly, but this thing I do not like.'

Weekly tried to think of her land again and what she would grow there. The sheds too, she had never had sheds and all the things people put in them. She wondered about the house. She wished she had asked to see inside it. She wondered where the tenant's wife would go when she, Weekly, the Newspaper of Claremont Street, bought the land.

'It is the music I miss so much.' Nastasya's voice penetrated the dream. 'But what would some one ignorant like you are Veekly know about Beethoven and the anguish of his last five quartets. What could you know about the caution and melancholy of the cello? Ah! cello, cello, cello! It is yet another terrible bereavement for me.' Nastasya began to wail aloud.

'Hold yer noise', Weekly muttered. 'Narsty, hold yer noise.' Weekly felt more and more, in some strange way, claimed by Nastasya. It was as if Nastasya was regarding Weekly as the person next to and closest to her simply because she had no other person. And if one human being claims another then this other is, in a sense, bound by this claim to belong.

The end of Nastasya's proud life was bound to be a sad one, but of course it was not the end yet. Who could tell when the end would be. Nastasya somehow seemed as if she would live for ever, even though she sat saying she had no strength so that Weekly had to do everything for her.

Weekly felt she must not fail Nastasya. It seemed to her that not failing people was what counted in her life and in the lives of others. Sometimes Weekly was afraid she was on the brink of some tremendously revealing truth. She was afraid to come upon the truth, because after that there could be nothing else.

'If yo' find out why youm livin',' her mother said once, 'if yo' find out *why* about anything like living, then as soon

68

as yo've found out, you drop dead.' 'Shut up Margie!', her mother said. 'Shut up Margie, stop arskin' so many questions. If yo' know too much yo' won't live long!' So Weekly did not search too deeply into the claim she felt from Nastasya.

'Torben, he love music, he could not live without, but where in this beeg empty country, which has no soul, where is there any music!' Nastasya stopped wailing after a time. And when Weekly looked at Nastasya it was clear she had been at her wicker trunk again, for she was now dressed in an assortment of old clothes, some loose trousers and an embroidered blouse with a belt, things which belonged to another time and another country. And, like a dirty pancake on the side of her face and head, was a white beret.

'Veekly,' Nastasya said flourishing a long cigarette holder, 'get me a drink please, I would like a drink with a gentle colour'. And as she walked towards Weekly, something about the way she walked increased the threat.

-10-

'Chatham's girl's back.' Weekly sank on to the broken chair and leaned on the counter to rest. The shop at the end of Claremont Street was full, everyone turned from their contemplation of kerosene and biscuits and cornflakes; there was plenty of time for staring for Val and Cheryl were the slowest shop assistants in the world. Often the people served themselves and the part behind the counter was as crowded as the shop. Too many people put things on the scales at once, and they often found themselves blocking the narrow spaces in the storeroom, sometimes being unable to move in or out.

It was a very short time since Weekly had described the wedding, the food and the presents and the well-dressed people who had travelled for miles for the occasion. She had been able to name all the expensive hotels where they had stayed.

'I wouldn't stay in one of them places if yo' paid me', Weekly said.

'Oh go on Newspaper,' Val nudged Cheryl, 'you would!'

'I like to know what's in me food.'

'Anyway what's wrong with Chatham's girl. Why is she back?'

Weekly had washed up at the engagement party a whole year ago and then three weeks ago she had washed up for hours at the wedding. Mrs Chatham had wanted the wedding at their home and it had been a splendid affair with photographs in the paper and a long paragraph of description. Leila Chatham was a pale girl and she had come back paler than ever, hollow-eyed and unable to eat. That morning she was sitting in the kitchen when Weekly stepped indoors. She was wearing a blue dressing gown made for her trousseau by her mother.

'Well 'ow are we?', Weekly called and the girl turned her pale sad face towards her, she tried to smile but her mouth trembled and tears hung on her lashes.

'Well, well, this will never do!' Weekly began to tear the stove to pieces.

'Either stop in bed or get dressed', Mrs Chatham said sharply to her daughter, she had no patience with nerves or hysteria, and she was desperately afraid her daughter couldn't manage married life and so had come home to mother.

'She says she's got a sore throat', Mrs Chatham explained with the impatience of fear to Weekly.

'Pore girl!' Weekly crashed the enamel pieces into the steaming detergent. 'There's a lot of that about. Now yo' should go back in bed, there's a good girl, and wrap an old stocking round yor neck. It's the best thing for a throat. A worn stocking not a washed one.'

'Yes Leila you do what Weekly says.' Mrs Chatham felt comforted by Weekly's advice, the only trouble was there was never anything unwashed in her house. Leila trailed quietly out of the kitchen.

The people in the shop waited for Weekly.

'Well, she's picked up this terrible germ up North and it's lodged in her body. She looks that sick!' Weekly shook her head. 'She always was a delicate girl and pore Mrs Chatham's gone crazy with worry. There's no cure for some

71

of them germs there is about up North.'

'Is her husband with her?' they wanted to know.

'No one's allowed near her,' Weekly said. 'Can't even go to the 'orspital, too dangerous! It'll be a miracle if she gets over it. Pore girl and pore Mrs Chatham!'

There was a sad silence in the shop as everyone began again to wonder what they had come for and Weekly sat on resting before giving out more intimate details of the Chatham household. Pauses now and then made each tiny piece of news more impressive, especially if Weekly hesitated as to whether she should tell it or not.

Every Sunday Weekly went out to look at the valley. And in the evenings Nastasya wept aloud, telling Weekly about a great river, ridged with swiftly flowing currents and foaming in flood, and how she had to cross it once with her Father, in a boat, when she was a child.

'I had such beautiful warm clothes, Veekly, and boots and soft furs to keep out the cold. I stood beside my Fazere and watched the brown waters gallopp-ing like horses without riders — you Veekly, can have no idea of such a river. And you can have no idea of the smell of the snow melting. If only I can see once more the little rivers shining like glass as the snow melts in spring. In this ugly country there is no spring, it is so ugly here!'

'If it was all that wonderful there,' Weekly muttered to herself, 'why don't yo'm go back where you belong'.

Weekly was sorry for Nastasya and she brought her some wildflowers stolen from the edge of the road. But Nastasya pushed aside the fragile little bunch. She was in a disagreeable mood.

'Kangaroo Paw, Veekly, is only beautiful when the sun is shining through the red and green velvet of it and you see it all lit up in among the trees and leaves in the bush. Don't bring me flowers!'

So then Weekly began to take Nastasya out to the valley, even though she would have preferred to go alone. As soon as Nastasya saw the valley she discovered a whole long hedge of wild, white roses. Sometimes she would notice

72

things like this after being wrapped up in dismal memories for days on end. Another time it seemed as if sheep were on the hillside among the pig-sties, but when they climbed up, they saw it was only the way the light came through the trees onto some greyish bushes, making them look like a quiet flock of sheep.

Suddenly Nastasya was happy in the fresh air and she kept telling Weekly, laughing and telling and enjoying, 'I feel so free Veekly! You cannot know how good I feel!'

And Weekly felt even more she was caught looking after Nastasya and having to be with her. Nastasya, who had seemed so weak, now had more strength than Weekly. She could even run up the hill and all the way back down without getting out of breath and Weekly was afraid she would have to have her for ever. 'What if she lives longer than me', she thought grimly to herself. At all the places where she worked everyone had someone else, but for some reason Nastasya had no one. While Torben was alive they had each other, and it must have been enough for them, and they never bothered about other people, either to know them or to help them. And so, without Torben, and the world they fabricated between them, Nastasya really did have no one and nothing. Weekly had as many people as she wanted while she was working and then after her work she liked to be alone.

Even though Nastasya seemed better and stronger she never helped with anything and insisted that Weekly prepare food for her as she liked it, and she insisted on being waited on.

'I am hongry Veekly', Nastasya said on the way home from the valley. 'It is the fresh air makes me so hongry.' So Weekly stopped beside the tottering verandah posts of a shabby shop.

'I want a milkshakes please, strawberries flavour.' Weekly went inside and bought biscuits for Nastasya.

'There's no strawberry', she said coming out to the car patiently. 'Will yo' have a lime? Lime's nice. I've brought you lime.'

'No I do not like. I like only strawberries flavour! I will

try raspberries, do they have raspberries flavour?'

Weekly never spent her money on things like this and she had to make an effort to stop thinking of the black cavity such a purchase would make in the steep silvery side of the money mountain. Nastasya took the packet into her lap and tore off the coloured paper and began to eat the biscuits greedily, one after the other. And then she said, 'I am hongry Veekly, but not for biscuits!'

Wearily Weekly thought as she drove home at dusk that she would have to boil potatoes and onions and leeks and, as Nastasya didn't eat them just boiled as she did, she would have to stand pushing them through a sieve and make the soup which was Nastasya's favourite.

'At home we had such a cook!' Nastasya sat in the only comfortable chair while Weekly worked. 'If you could only see how the soup was this cook made for us you would see what it should really be like.' Nastasya stretched out her flabby legs. See how sittink in the car makes for me the swollen feet. Oh my poor feet!' Weekly tried to take no notice of Nastasya's lamenting voice.

'I would like some borscht', Nastasya wailed. 'You have no idea even what it is! Our cooks, Veekly, had such wonderful recipes but they were never written down.' She lowered her voice. 'No recipe Veekly for cake or soup, or any sauce or dish was ever written down in case someone steal it!' She paused. 'Our cooks Veekly', Nastasya said, 'made all food from their own heads!'

For some reason the smell of the potatoes boiling made Weekly remember the children, when she was a child herself, sliding down the stone balustrades of the band stand in the East Park.

'Margie yo'um not to play with any of those children', her mother had called out after her when she went out to play. She never said why the children shouldn't be played with.

'Perhaps it's because they've got the fever', Victor said to his sister. But Margie thought it was because they went about with no knickers on, but of course she couldn't say

74

this to her brother. He was frightened of the fever hospital and always ran past the high walls holding his nose. They often tried to frighten each other at dusk saying a fever man was dangling over the wall to drop on them and give them the fever.

As she sieved the soup for Nastasya, Weekly thought she would go ahead and buy some land. She had enough money saved up. She would either have to put Nastasya into a hospital or nursing-home or take her with her. She would have to decide quite soon what to do and she felt the burden of this.

In the night Nastasya was ill.

'I am dyink Veekly fetch Doctor quick.'

'What's wrong Narsty?' Weekly slowly and painfully got off her bed, she always began her aching during the night; it was not just a thing of the morning. Her body ached all over, it was hardly possible to move.

'God moves in a mysterious way', she sang, forcing herself to get up.

'Do not, I implore you, make so much noise!' Nastasya clutched herself and rolled about, moaning, all her bed clothes were on the floor. Slowly Weekly remade her bed.

'Don't leave me Veekly', Nastasya implored. 'Fetch Doctor or else I die in an hour' — this was a contradiction and a mixed threat.

Weekly set off slowly in the dark. Never mind if Nastasya had quarrelled with the doctors in Claremont Street; she couldn't go farther in the dark and her aching had not been cured by sweeping the verandah.

'I'll get old Muttonhead', she said to herself, groaning as she went. 'And tomorrer I'll take her to the hospital!'

When at last she returned with the doctor, Nastasya behaved with great charm. She had put on a bedjacket and she stretched out her hand to the doctor as if she were a hostess at a party. Weekly fidgetted in the corners of her room, grumbling and muttering and glaring at Nastasya for what she had done.

'Eet is nothing Doctor. I was sufferink from some bad

cookink. I am quite all right now. Just someone cook very badly and I have terrible pain because of it. But I am perfectly well now. Thank you for comink out in the night, poor Doctor Darlink! Is quite unnecessary. Gut night.'

'Thank you, I will let myself out', the Doctor said coldly to Weekly.

'That was wicked of you Narsty. Very wicked!' Weekly, tired and cross, sat heavily into her bed. She hadn't wanted to call anyone out in the night, least of all someone from Claremont Street. She could have shaken Nastasya, but what was the use.

'It's no use!', she muttered. 'It's no use at all.' Her face was very grim, she resolved to get rid of Nastasya the next day; there was no reason at all why she should keep her and look after her.

'You know Veekly that Doctor is just like our coachman back home, a kind of bear, quite good natured but stupid. Only in this country can he be Doctor, back home just a coachman!' She laughed and she must have seen Weekly's expression for she stopped laughing at once and began crying. At first Weekly thought she was pretending to cry but her face was all wet with tears.

'Oh I am so ashamed of myself Veekly', she cried bitterly. 'Oh I am so ashamed. You are so good to me and I am so bad!' She cried so much Weekly got off the bed and crossed over the room to comfort her.

'Never mind Narsty', she said at the bedside. 'Just you hold yer noise now and try an' go to sleep', and quite suddenly Nastasya fell asleep, touchingly like a little child with the tears still on her eye lashes. And Weekly went back to bed as quietly as she could.

In spite of being tired Weekly could not sleep; thoughts from times long ago came crowding into her mind.

Victor was unwell; he had sent a message asking her to come. She was used to such messages. She dreaded the appearance of the urchin at the backdoor with his declaration that he had a letter for M. Morris and not anybody else but her. This happened too often and Weekly lived in fear of her

Lady in the Big House finding out and asking, 'What is it Morris? Who has come to the house?'

Often while she washed the steps, Weekly tried to invent explanations to store in her head should any questions be asked when the boy, appearing from nowhere, asked for her.

'What is it Morris? Who has come to see you? What is it Morris? A letter? Who from?'

'It's the boy from the laundry Ma'am. I'm sorry I forgot the list Ma'am. It's a message from my sister, Ma'am, 'er wants me to go over on me half day, Ma'am.'

Weekly's private life did not excite the household and no one, not even the other servants, ever questioned. The boy, however, on every occasion, slipped away with a small but precious coin tight in his dirty hand, paid by Weekly to keep his silence.

As soon as she could, after receiving such a message, she would set off walking to whichever place it was where Victor had an apartment. Because his address was always different he had to send a boy with a letter so that she would know where to come.

All through the years Weekly carried in her mind a picture of Victor which she had never seen. The picture was so vivid it was as though she knew exactly what happened every time Victor sent her one of his letters. She imagined him frail and coughing painfully, wrapped up, leaning out of an upstairs window desperately trying to attract the attention of an idle boy, to call him from the gutter to come up and carry a letter for him quick, 'quick as you can boy take this letter. . . .' And then, banging the window shut, he would disappear from sight. That was how she imagined him and she knew the reality was bronchitis.

She found him in bed in pain, she thought, with his familiar illness. Quickly she filled the kettle to ease him with steam.

'No no! You fool! I don't need you to boil a kettle', he was impatient with her. 'I'm on the mend. I'm hungry. I haven't eaten for days. What have you brought me?' He sat up in bed gathering the quilt around him.

Weekly noticed at once that the room was shabby, not at all like the previous apartments where he had all the fashionable luxuries and where his clients could feel at ease and have confidence in him because of his wealth.

His pale fingers tore the white cloth from the little veal and ham pies she had taken from the pantry. 'These are cold!', he pushed them away in disgust.

'I didn't have the chance to heat 'em,' she whispered, 'I aven't got the afternoon orf, only a hour. I 'ave to be back to the Nursery by half three!' Not listening to her and, without grace or gratitude, he pulled the other things out of her basket. She had spent her hard-earned wages recklessly, on the way to him, on white rolls and pâté and a soft creamy cheese.

'Peaches, that's better,' he bit into the fragrant, expensive flesh and quickly finished the fruit. 'Only two?'

'Them's expensive', she apologized, watching him.

'This wine's no good, no good at all', he held up the ornamental bottle she had chosen for him. 'Remember, it's champagne I need when I'm ill; this bubbling pearl, or whatever it is, is just soapsuds as far as I'm concerned.'

Victor drank some of the wine and Weekly was pleased to see some colour come into his fragile face.

'Ugh! Soapsuds!' He made a face at the wine.

'Yo'll be better soon', she wanted to comfort him.

'I'll have to be', he said, 'I'm just waiting for my passport and I'm off to South Africa. But it's not your business to know where I'm going or why. And it's nobody's business either to know. I'm lying up here till I feel stronger and then I'm off, as soon as my papers are through.'

He looked about him with a distaste, which included Weekly. She looked away from him, hurt.

'This place is disgusting,' he said, 'I'll be gone before the rent's due. Have you brought what else I asked for?'

Reluctantly she laid what remained of her small wealth on the bed.

'Is this all. This can't be all?' She thought he was angry enough to shake her. Quickly his nimble fingers, accustomed, tossed through the money counting it.

'On no account give Victor money', their mother had said to Weekly more than once.

As she lay in bed, sleepless, she remembered how on the way back to the Big House that afternoon she kept wishing she had said something more to comfort Victor. She wished she had kissed him like she sometimes, in those days, kissed his faded childhood photograph. Their mother had often explained to her that Victor could not help being disagreeable. He was like he was because of how their world was. The world was cruel and ugly, she had said, and people like Victor could see this, they knew what people were like and knew what they were like themselves but did not know how to say what they knew and saw.

Weekly groaned aloud with the bitter pain of memory. That afternoon was the last time she ever saw Victor. Every time she thought about it all the years later, and she did think often, she wished she could have the afternoon again and somehow do things differently and somehow un-say some of the things she had said. She was about half-way home when a smartly dressed man had stopped beside her.

'Miss Morris?', he had said there in the street. Weekly groaned aloud, Nastasya stirred.

'What is it Veekly. You have pain?', she asked sleepily in the dark.

'No, I'm orl right, get orf to sleep!'

What was the use thinking like this, there was nothing she could do now. She waited a while till she was sure Nastasya was fast asleep again and she put on her light. Weekly reached for her old school reading book. There were a few poems in the back part. There was part of one she liked, she didn't know who had written it. She read the verse aloud, softly for herself, catching her breath, reading carefully as if she were back at school reading in the classroom

'All things that love the sun are out of doors,
The sky rejoices in the morning's birth;

79

The grass is bright with rain drops; — on the moors
The Hare is running races in her mirth;
And with her feet she from the plashy earth
Raises a mist, that, glittering in the sun,
Runs with her all the way, where ever she doth run.'

That was what her money was. And, as she began to sink into her cradle, fragrant with thought of the silver figures adding and growing, the total changing as if on a little gilt-edged board, like a plaything on the side of the cradle she thought, and the thought comforted her. Of all the land she had seen, the valley was the most beautiful, and it was what she wanted. She would go as soon as possible and buy the valley.

– 11 –

Sometimes lately, the Newspaper of Claremont Street came home from her work by way of an old lane which was behind the houses, a neglected path reminding of times gone by. Tall grass grew there and enormous old oleanders. They were like big coloured skirts embroidered with pink and white flowers and threaded with the blue-cupped bindweed. In places the lane had disappeared because of new buildings and car parks, but it was possible to have quite a tranquil walk, especially towards the back of the bottom end of the street where less alterations had taken place. It was when she walked through the lane that Weekly remembered the sky and looked at it. Mostly she forgot about it and, when she thought of looking up between the massed oleanders, taking care not to trip over bits of wood and rubble in the grass and not go headlong over an old push-chair or a dustbin, she saw with reverence and renewed pleasure the greatness of the sky.

'Red sky at night, the shepherd's delight.'

Her Father always looked at the sky and talked about it,

'Red sky in the morning, shepherd's warning.'

Weekly could quote this without really knowing what it meant. Her Father always noticed the air, the freshness of it and the fine soft caress of the morning on his face. For days on end Weekly forgot about the air. In the lane she thought of it and the loveliness of it reminded her of the strength and beauty of her money. It was now a considerable sum but, as she walked, she tried to get over the shock she had had this afternoon. She tried to look at the clouds. There were so many kinds of clouds, her Father had known them all. She tried to remember them now. Cumulus and cirrus, then there was nimbus, the rain-bearing cloud, but the mackerel sky was the one she pictured best and, for a moment, she could remember the sky ribbed all over as if with the firm white flesh, tinged delicately with pink, of a fish. Once her Mother cooked a mackerel and her Father was sick all night and the cat died.

Cumulus, cirrus, nimbus and mackerel, even if she talked to herself saying over the names of the clouds she found she was unable to see them. The sky suddenly seemed overcast by her own thoughts. She began to hurry through the lane. There was nothing to remind her of her money. She scarcely saw the oleanders and did not notice when she stubbed her foot on a piece of old railway sleeper, thrown carelessly across the path. She walked fast leaning forward, her skirts swirling in the coming dusk.

'Hi Newspaper!', the boys called her from the corner when she came into Claremont Street. 'What's happening in the world? What's the news?', but she ignored them and went across into the shop and sank onto the broken chair, propping herself on the counter.

'What about a lottery ticket?', Val called across the shop but Weekly could not be bothered to pick up the little coloured book of flimsy pages, one of which might be a number on which she would save a dollar, by not buying it.

'Go on Weekly buy a ticket, big prizes!' Cheryl came and leaned her plump bosom on the sheets of newspaper they used for wrapping beans and lettuces. 'What's the news?' she asked. Weekly pulled herself together. She sucked in her cheeks and narrowed her eyes and looked around the shop to see how many people were there; no use to tell news to nothing except the floorboards, dark with kerosene, and littered just now with rhubarb leaves and the rotten bits pulled off vegetables.

'You buyin' a cool drink?' Weekly looked up and down a well-dressed woman who was close to the counter.

'No.'

'Well what yo' taken two drinking straws for then?'

It was disconcerting for customers to have their small robberies noticed. After a pause Weekly said, 'Pore Mr Kingston!', she shook her head and addressed the shop. 'I done the whole of 'is puzzle terday. Mr Kingston, I said, let Aunty do yer crorssword', she paused again to suck in her cheeks. 'There was not one word he could fill in 'imself. I doubt he'll leave his bed again', she said.

Silence fell among the groceries and the women and their last-minute shopping. The silence remained unbroken, for Weekly had stopped talking; her own thoughts were too much for her and they took over and prevented her from going on with her gossip. Her mind was occupied with thinking of the valley. She seemed to see the wooded slope and the bright meadow, small as if on a postcard; it was so vivid she forgot what she was talking about. For the first time her thoughts of the valley were sad and troubled.

All her savings, her gilded cone-shaped mountain of money, her cradle of comfortable silver, were not enough, not enough even for part of the meadow. The valley was quite beyond her reach, the land was far too valuable and far too expensive. She was trying, as during her walk through the lane, to get over the terrible disappointment she had just had. And of course, since she had never spoken about it to anyone she could not talk of it now.

She had taken an hour off to keep an appointment with Mr Rusk the land agent. She sat in his brown office and a beam of afternoon sun lay across his leather-topped desk, showing up the dust, but Weekly scarcely noticed it.

'If you're prepared to go out, say fifty miles,' Mr Rusk said gently, 'at a little place called White Gum Crossing, near there, there's a nice five acres with a tin shack for tools. Some of it's what they call river flats, flooded in winter, you could grow pears there. And it would be within your price range,' Mr Rusk spoke seriously to the old woman even though he was not sure whether she was all right in the head. 'Think it over', he advised. He always regarded a customer as a buyer until the customer did not buy.

As she sat in the shop Weekly tried to forget her valley. She began in her mind to scatter the new land with pear blossom. It was not easy but she was used, all her life, to making an effort, and now, with great effort, she disciplined her thoughts. She would go out there as soon as she could.

'Goodnight all!', she left the shop abruptly without telling any news at all.

It was some weeks before Weekly was able to go, on a Sunday, to look at the five acres. The days were hot now and the country was brown and dried up and, though cattle grazed, it was hard to see what they could possibly find to eat in the bald paddocks. She had to leave much later in the day than she wanted to because there was Nastasya in her wood-block mood and everything had to be done for her; pulling on her wrinkled stockings, fastening her shoes and her dress, combing her hair and even holding a cup to her lips to make her drink some tea. When Nastasya was like this Weekly came near to despair. How could she ever do any of the things she wanted to do?

The car required little attention since it had been so thoroughly overhauled, but Weekly always spent a few minutes going over the engine with a duster. She made an odd sight every day when she opened the bonnet of the old car. In her mended clothes, the darns and stitching like embroidery in strange places, she awkwardly leaned into the engine, peering and polishing before setting off with a crash of gears and her foot kept too long and too hard down on the clutch.

84

At last she arrived at the place. It was more lovely than she had expected and fragrant and quite different from the valley. This difference gave her a surprise. A great many tall old trees had been left standing, white gums and red gums and jarrah, and the tin shack turned out to be a weatherboard cottage. She was afraid she had come to the wrong place.

'It must be someone's home,' she thought to herself as she peered timidly through the cottage window and saw that it was full of furniture. Disappointment crept over her as she turned away stepping on the purple pigface which was growing everywhere. She climbed the broken steps at the back of the cottage and, from the high verandah, she looked down the sunlit slope of the land and across a narrow valley to a hay field between big trees. It was like the things she had read about, only far more beautiful because of the stillness and fragrance. These are not put into the advertisements. There was such a stillness that Weekly felt more than ever she was trespassing, not only on the land, but into the very depths of the stillness itself.

On the verandah was a home-made sofa, the lumpy mattress was tucked over with a rough woollen blanket. Weekly sat down on it, she felt tired. It was the long drive and the excitement of coming, and then the feeling that it was the wrong place, and that it all belonged to someone else and could not be hers. On the table beside the sofa was a piece of candle stuck on a saucer. In the heat of the afternoon, the candle began slowly to bow to her.

She woke up about an hour later. It was unusual for her to sleep during the day, she was not used to it. She woke as a little child wakes in a strange place, crying, tears streamed down her thin wrinkled cheeks and she cried aloud for her mother as if she was a little girl again. Her wailing broke the stillness.

'Now stop that or I'll give yer summat to cry for!', her own voice in the middle of her tears surprised her; her mother would have said it. She supplied the words herself sharply, and the quietness, after all her noise, was all at once filled with birds. Black cockatoos left the tree tops in twos and threes and then in their numbers and came swirling in ever widening circles, screaming and calling in their flight. The shallow ravine of trees and the endless stretches of trees and scrub on either side of the piece of land seemed full of these birds. Their heads were round and determined and black fringes edged their wings and, as they flew round and through the trees, they brought to the place a quality of strangeness, of something unknown, as if they had some other knowledge, something to do with another kind of life.

'I must be orf home', Weekly muttered to herself as the screaming subsided. She was not used to such a loneliness and she had never seen in her life such a flock of birds. And she hobbled down the broken steps quickly and started back up the track to where she had left the car.

The light was fading from the northern hills and a wind came along the valley, only a small wind; it was a soft, deep roar among the branches of the trees. Weekly turned back to see the trees swaying, she heard the wind before she felt it.

'The voice of the Lord moveth the cedar tops'

she said and went on as quickly as she could, though she would have liked to stay longer.

'I got that wrong', she said to herself in the car. "ow does it go, the wind in the trees reminded me', she thought to herself. 'Aw yes!

'The voice of the Lord is powerful'

that's it!

'The voice of the Lord'

Weekly sang aloud in the car.

'The voice of the Lord breaketh the cedars yea,
the Lord breaketh the cedars,

well I hope He don't talk too loud and break them trees back up there!', and with her mind full of the Twenty-ninth Psalm she reached the outskirts of the city and drove through a red light she was so busy thinking.

86

Mr Rusk said it was the five acres he had meant, he assured her there was no mistake.

'I've never been there myself,' he explained when she told him about the cottage. She tried to describe to him the silence and the privacy and she told him about the big old trees standing so still with the secrets of their years.

He listened to her with polite kindness.

'Yes,' he said, 'there is some standing timber, quite remarkable, as most of the jarrah was taken from that area years ago'.

'It is the place', he said. 'Everything's included in the price, leaves you something over for extras too', he smiled at the strange old woman who had laid her small wealth before him and asked his advice anxiously and with a trust he had never seen before in all his experience of buying and selling.

So Weekly tried to stop thinking of the valley so much and every Sunday she began to go to the five acres. She walked down the slope over the fragrant warm earth scattered with leaves and twigs, and peered into the cottage trying to see as much as she could of the inside through the tiny windows. She walked back up the slope, caressed by the light and shade, wondering how long the trees had been there.

Left to herself more than usual and for longer than usual Nastasya had done several crazy things. Once she had dressed herself in some tattered remains of her national costume and had gone out scattering her money on the pavement, trying to give it to people who just stared at her. And then she had taken a taxi to the station and, as she had no money left, she gave the taxi driver Torben's ring. Then, just as Weekly was falling asleep, tired out, Nastasya began to weep and howl.

'Veekly! My Ring. Torben's Ring from his Mother. I must have it. Please Veekly! go out and find the taxi and get from him my ring. Veekly I beg you!' She made so much noise Weekly was afraid the people in the other rooms would hear and be disturbed and annoyed.

'Oh hush Narsty do!', she said and, while she got

dressed, she grumbled and complained to herself, her complaining voice made a kind of background music to Nastasya's shrill lamenting.

She returned about two hours later, unsuccessful, fearful of how Nastasya would be about her failure to find the ring only to find Nastasya was fast asleep. Furthermore Nastasya forgot about the ring completely for she never spoke of it again.

Whenever Weekly was on her way home she was worried that Nastasya might have done something really dreadful in her absence.

– 12 –

One Sunday Weekly sat longer on the verandah of the little cottage. She had made up her mind to buy the land and, as she sat there alone, she felt it was already hers. She watched the trees change to a dark embroidery of lace on the yellowing sky of the dusk. A heron flew alone searching for food, its slow flight adding to the enchantment of the evening. Reluctantly Weekly left the lonely place.

It was quite dark when she reached her room in the old house in Claremont Street. This time Weekly found her room quite changed. Nastasya had decorated the drab walls with strips of paper, festoons of it fell as Weekly opened the door. The table was spread with cups and plates and there was a packet of nuts and a little dish with biscuits. A bottle of sweet sherry stood in the middle.

'Veekly I invite for party tonight', Nastasya came forward, flour dropping from her hands.

'You are josst in time', she said. 'See I make cake,' she explained. 'With yeast!' Round her head was a crazy garland of paper flowers. They were cut out from an old newspaper, folded and fringed, it must have taken Nastasya a long time to make them.

Weekly was very tired after the long drive and she needed her meal. Rage rose in her.

'Narsty take orf those clothes this minute. Yo' can't wear them things. Yo' can see right through them! There's no party here. This is my place, you understand? Just you look at all this mess you've made!' She picked up some of the paper, and with her floor cloth, she began to wipe up the flour.

'I invite you Veekly!, and I invite my Doctor and my Lawyer and my Benk Menecher he is very nice men Veekly, you will like and I invite all of my Friends. You will see. Beeg Fun Time!' Nastasya danced a few steps of an obscure traditional dance, her hip caught the corner of the table and crockery and cutlery cascaded. The wine rolled to a corner.

'Oh my Gawd!' Weekly rummaged in the flyscreen cupboard and brought out her food. It was very hot and airless in the room. She tried not to look at the mess. She would clear up a bit later on.

'Leetle glass of sherry Veekly?' Nastasya retrieved the bottle. She pulled the piece of dirty chiffon she had pinned into a kind of dress up on to her shoulder, the thin material kept slipping down so that she was almost naked. The paper flowers flopped over one eye, giving her a drunken irresponsible appearance. 'But first I must say my Tischgebet, Grace you know Veekly.' Nastasya paused with the bottle in one hand. Weekly began to eat hungrily.

'Vait Veekly!', Nastasya commanded, Weekly had to stop chewing, she sat still with her mouth full. 'When I was a child Veekly,' Nastasya said, 'I had a German governess, a Fraulein you understand, such a silly dumpling, she was afraid of earthworms, can you imagine! She taught me Grace, I will bless our feast–Liebe Herr Jesu sei unser Gast und segne was Duuns bescherest hast–oi vey!' Nastasya adjusted her paper wreath and made a face at herself in the mirror over the mantelpiece. 'Now! Leetle glass of sherry Veekly. My Fraulein was not my Nurse you know Veekly, they was

90

separate peoples. My Nurse I love very much!'

Weekly and Nastasya sipped their sherry and every time Nastasya heard a car in Claremont Street she rushed to the window to peer out in to the darkness to see if it was a guest to her party. The evening crept by and no guests came. The old house was its usual forgotten, secretive self; all the people who lived there quietly going about their own affairs till it was time to sleep.

Nastasya became more and more dejected as time went by and she wailed in a hoarse voice, saying things in her own language which Weekly could not understand.

'How's about bed Narsty old Thing?' Weekly suggested at last. She was deeply sorry for Nastasya. No one had come to the party, no doctor, no lawyer, no bank manager and of course, no friends. What friend did Nastasya have other than Weekly.

Nastasya made more noise than ever, weeping; she was heart-broken, she cried aloud, she couldn't remember the name of her Nurse. 'Perhaps she didn't have no name, praps you just called her Nursie', Weekly tried to comfort Nastasya. She tried to quieten her, 'Hush yer noise Narsty, the whole house will hear yo'. Hush yer noise, do!' She thought she would help Nastasya to bed. But Nastasya was a heavy woman and she slid to the floor taking Weekly down with her. Weekly found herself, much to her surprise, holding Nastasya across her lap with her arms round her, tangled in the strip of chiffon. In this moment of tenderness, which was strange and unaccustomed, Weekly cradled Nastasya's grey head against her own hard flat chest. And then Weekly sang to Nastasya to soothe her.

'There is a fountain filled with blood',

she sang. In an attempt to soften her voice into a lullaby she found the sounds came out cracked and out of tune but Nastasya was quite uncritical.

'There is a fountain filled with blood',

Weekly sang.

'Drawn from Emmanuel's veins,
And sinners plunged beneath that flood
Lose all their guilty stains.'

Over and over again she sang

'There is a fountain filled with blood'

rocking Nastasya to and fro, gently trying to comfort her. As
she sat there Weekly thought about the five acres. More than
anything she wanted to be there alone. She was used to being
alone except when she was working. Whatever could she do
about Nastasya.

She looked at Nastasya, she had at last gone to sleep
after Weekly had managed to put her on to her bed. She was
still swathed in the old chiffon though Weekly had carefully
removed the pins. Whatever could she do about Nastasya. She
wanted to buy the five acres and she wanted to be there
alone. She resolved to take Nastasya to the hospital as soon
as she could.

Giving up Nastasya was in no way the same as the giving
up of Victor all those years ago. It was for Nastasya's good;
the hospital had people who could cure her and look after
her in ways quite beyond Weekly's ability.

What she had done to Victor was quite different and she
was quite unable to forgive herself, even though at the time,
Victor's ways were beyond her understanding, and his needs
were far beyond anything she could provide.

'It's not your business to know where I'm going, it's
nobody's business, either, to know', Victor's well-spoken
voice was always clear in her mind. If only she did not
remember that afternoon so much. When she had left him
with the little store of food and all the money she possessed,
she had walked quickly along the pavement. She was worried
because she knew she would be late back. There were trees at
intervals, and as she came to every tree in turn, some sweet-
scented blossom refreshed her. She tried to take pleasure in
the fragrance but Victor's voice and his threatening request,
as she was leaving, worried her.

Coldly, in his well-bred accents, so different from her own way of speaking, but entirely the Victor from their childhood, he told her that she must get hold of a hundred pounds and bring it to him the next day, even if she had to steal it.

Their mother had stolen for Victor. Weekly never had. She was frightened. She liked her work, they were good to her at the Big House. She liked the children, was quite fond and proud of them if she took them for a walk when their nurse was busy.

As she thought about the money Victor wanted she knew she simply could not take it from those people. Wildly, she imagined herself asking if she could borrow a hundred pounds.

'A hundred pounds Morris? That's a great deal of money. Could I ask why you want it?' As she tried to think up answers she might give in reply to expected questions she felt helpless.

'Miss Morris?' the smartly dressed young man, about Victor's age she guessed, stepped from behind one of the scented trees. He stood squarely in front of her on the pavement.

'Miss Morris?' It was a shock, because no one ever called her that.

'Yes,' she said before she was able to think of saying 'no'.

'Ah! I thought so,' he smiled warmly, 'you are so like your brother! May I walk with you a little?' He held out his arm to her. Weekly, unaccustomed, did not know how to take his arm. Gently he drew her hand and arm through his, and holding her hand firmly with his other hand clasped over the top, he walked with her drawn close up to him. As ladies walked, Weekly reflected. Gently he propelled her along the pavements. All the time he smiled smoothly and talked, 'I'm a friend of your brother's,' he said, 'but the silly thing is—I've lost his address. Some of us, his friends, are trying to catch up with him. It's to his advantage, a business deal you know, nothing for a little lady to bother her pretty head about.' His charming smile was turned towards Weekly so that she blushed, an unusual thing for her, no one had ever said her head was pretty before. Nervously, but pleased, she smiled back at him. Not being little, but rather big, she smiled down towards his round slightly bulging eyes.

'I was just driving by when I saw you. The image of Victor! I said to myself—there's my car, by the way, over there on the corner. Hey! What about I take you for a little spin? Have you even been for a drive in a motor car? We'll drive round and see some more of Victor's friends. You'd like that I know.'

'Oh Sir, I should be back. I'm to be in the Nursery by half three,' she whispered.

'Oh it won't take a minute. I'll see you are back in time. Come on. Hop in!'

There were five young men in leather chairs around a horseshoe-shaped table. They sat Weekly in a deep spongy chair and asked her all kinds of questions. They had something for her brother they said. It was urgent that they find him. They kept repeating that it was to do with business, nothing that she should bother about, she need not even try to understand but it was very important for him that they find him. They said it was stupid of them to have lost his address.

'Aw! he's always movin',' Weekly said, 'one place one minnit, gorn the next!'

Flattered by the attention of so many young men and the importance of being Victor's sister and, furthermore, being told that she looked like Victor, Weekly told them about the shabby room. She told them where it was, and she told them,

'Yo'll 'ave to be quick as he's leavin' for South Africa in a day or two. It occurred to her that these friends could help Victor and free her from the burden of providing for him whenever his business, whatever it was, was in trouble of some sort. Cheerfully she answered their questions.

It was only when she was out in the summer-scented street again, clear of the immense room and the cigarette smoke and the smartly dressed, smooth-voiced young men that she realised what she had done. She was out in the street alone, the first young man had disappeared and no one else had taken any more notice of her. The light had changed; it was much later than she thought. The street was lined on both sides by old houses. Some of them, used as consulting rooms and business offices, had neglected overgrown gardens. A lost dog in a garden, which was no longer regarded as a garden, looked at her with mournful eyes. All at once she understood the questions. These men were not Victor's friends at all. She had given her cherished brother to people who had given nothing either to her or to Victor.

In spite of being burdened and hurt by Victor he was all she had, she loved him. In her thoughts on that afternoon and in all the years afterwards she knew that whatever Victor had taken from her, how-ever unkind or rude he had been he would never have given her away to anyone, and especially not to anyone like the false-faced man who had called her Miss Morris and had folded her arm into his so meaninglessly.

Frequently during the years, she relived in her imagination the horror of the moment when these men would have come upon Victor in his weak state in that sad, dirty room. Possibly while she was hurrying back to her work they had found the place where he was hiding. In her imagination she repeatedly heard his hoarse painful breathing and she would, in her mind, see his terrible shock at having five or six of them come to him, not for a good business deal but for some kind of revenge which she could not begin to understand or know about. All she could know and think about was that Victor was being hunted and, because of her, he would be trapped and caught.

As the first grey light filled the narrow space of her tall window, Weekly stared with disbelief at the waiting sky of the new day.

'Make my coffee Veekly! Make my coffee very strong and black and I wish my coffee packed with lemons', Nastasya's complaining voice stopped Weekly from dwelling on the thoughts which had been like an uncomfortable pillow for most of the night. She was so stiff and her body ached so much she thought she would never get to work, let alone take Nastasya to the hospital.

'Make my coffee Veekly!'

'You ever heard of sayin' "please" Narsty?'

For a moment she hoisted herself to the top of the shining mountain of coins. The mountain had grown again after the shock of its sudden smallness when compared to the cost of the valley. Mr Rusk had helped to rebuild it with the new land. 'It's well within your price range,' the cone of coins stretched up higher at once and its sides glittered. 'Leaves you something for extras, everything's included in the price.'

Slowly Weekly pushed her feet into her slippers and she hobbled across the room to put on the kettle; she would see Mr Rusk today and buy the land and, in her lunch time, she would take Nastasya to the hospital.

–13–

'Here's the Newspaper of Claremont Street', Valerie called out. 'Anyone been burned to death or drowned lately?', she asked. A few people were shopping as Weekly, tired out from an exceptional day, sank on to the broken chair.

'Ask old Muttonhead,' she said. 'He's followed me down to the shop. He'll be wanting toilet rolls and Bran.' The girls laughed and nudged each other.

'What about some news,' they said, 'anyone found naked in the park?'

'Well forty people was pulled from the surf Saturday, one drownded dead', Weekly sucked in her cheeks. 'And Sunday night there was a pile up of seven cars on the west highway', she paused and waited for attention from the other people who were shopping. 'Five people killed all from one family except for the little baby.' She seemed to sink into thought as a general sigh of dismay spread round the shop. 'Aw! the poor little baby!'

'How's Leila Chatham?' But Weekly had told her news for the day. Leila Chatham and the cure of daisy poultices, recommended by Weekly, could wait for another time. Mrs Chatham was covering Leila with hot stewed-up daisies, it was something remembered from the Black Country childhood.

'Well I suppose it can't do any harm', Mrs Chatham stood undecided in the hall.

'Buying land takes time', Mr Rusk had said gently, and so Weekly was containing herself in patience. 'Leave everything to me', Mr Rusk advised. 'I'll get the deed stamped and signed and there's a key to the building. I'll get that.'

Building seemed too vague a word for the delightfulness of the little house that would be Weekly's. She had patience and she could wait and she trusted Mr Rusk. She had squeezed in the appointment with him and had left the Laceys' a little early at lunch time in order to take Nastasya to the hospital.

'Tell about Sophie Whiteman', Diana Lacey tried to detain Weekly. Mrs Lacey had as usual gone to town and Diana was off school again, this time with a sore throat.

'Wash the curtains please.' Mrs Lacey felt this was a precaution against more illness. 'We must get rid of all the nasty germs,' she said, 'and Weekly I think the dining-room curtains need a bit of sewing—if you have time—thank you', and she had rushed off as she was late for the hairdresser.

'Well,' said Weekly putting away the ironing board, 'she got a pair of scissors and she went into the garding and she looked all about her to see no one was watching and she cut up a earth worm into a whole lot of little pieces'.

'What did her mother do?', asked Diana joyfully, knowing from a previous telling.

'Well,' said Weekly, 'she come in from town and she took orf her hat and her lovely fur coat, very beautiful lady, Mrs Whiteman, she took orf her good clothes and she took Sophie Whiteman and laid her acrorss her lap and give her a good hidin' '.

'Oh!', Diana was pleased. 'Was that before she died of the chocolate lining in her stomach or after?'

'Diana Lacey what have I told you before, remember?

Sophie Whiteman had her good hidin' afore she died. How could she cut up a worm after she was dead. Use yor brains!'

Weekly found a scrap of paper and scrawled a note for Mrs Lacey.

Will come early tomorrow to run up yor curtings M.M.

It had been a trying day as Weekly had hurried home in the lunch time. Mr Rusk had said she might have possession of the land in a week or a fortnight; he hoped it wouldn't be too long to wait. For Weekly, who had waited all her life for something, it was not long, but the burden of Nastasya lay heavily over the pleasure of the excitement of acquisition.

The mental hospital was within walking distance of Claremont Street. Some time earlier Weekly had gone there and described Nastasya to a doctor.

'Bring her along to be examined,' he said to her, 'and we'll see what we can do for her'.

At the time she meant to take Nastasya but somehow could not. Now she knew she must make up her mind.

'Come on Narsty,' Weekly said hurrying into the room in the middle of the day, a time when she usually did not go home, 'get dressed! We'll go for a little drive.' Weekly stood grim with intention in the dishevelled room. It annoyed her to have her room in the kind of mess Nastasya made. Nastasya began to put on her clothes quite quickly which was surprising as she had been in her wood-block mood for several weeks and her depression during the last few days had seemed to get worse.

'Vere ve go Veekly?', she asked with sudden pleasure. It would have been easier if she had stayed difficult and disagreeable. Weekly would have preferred to have to push her into her clothes and drag her out to the car. But Nastasya was pleased and happy.

'Oh how happy I am to go out!' she exclaimed, and her face was wrinkled with smiles. She waved to the people going by in Claremont Street and Weekly groaned inside herself as she drove round and round the park. Nastasya talked all the time and waved to people. 'You know Veekly a wise man called Plato, I don't think you will know of him, well he said this, while you are waitink to be born, because you know Veekly people hang in a kind of space waitink for to be born, well, while you are waitink to be born, if you could see the future course of your life and were given the chance to take it or not would you take it? Do you understand Veekly?'

'Yes o' course I do!' Weekly concentrated on a bend in the road; it was about the sixth time around the park.

'Well', Nastasya continued. 'It is like ziss if I had the choice and if I saw this park as it is today in spite of all the dreadful suffering in my life Veekly, because of this after-noon only, and you taking me out in the car, I would choose to have my awful, awful life just because of this afternoon!'

Weekly took the car once more around the park. She knew what Nastasya meant. She drove her back to the room in the house in Claremont Street to go on as before.

'I see soap powder's gorn up, and bread, whatever next!' Weekly was late to the Kingstons' and was late all afternoon and slammed about in the kitchen for she never liked to be all behind herself. She was so fierce with the stove that Mrs Kingston had to go and lie down somewhere quiet and as far away from the kitchen as possible.

No one knew about Weekly's troubles for, though she talked all the time about all sorts of things, she never spoke about her land, and she never told about Nastasya.

All the week she wondered how she could get Nastasya to the hospital. She wanted to get Nastasya settled before she received the key to the cottage. She found she could think of nothing else. She had stopped reading advertisements.

'I must be going out of me mind', she muttered to herself while she ate her bread and vegetables. She forced herself to take up the paper. She wanted to read the advertisements to see the prices to compare with what she would be paying for hers, to see if Mr Rusk had cheated her in any way. But she couldn't concentrate on the reading, she scarcely heard what Nastasya was saying though, every evening, her voice went on and on.

Tables set with embroidered cloths and heavy silver and

with glasses and decanters, so elegant and finely made that a kind of delicate music came from them when they were handled, and expensively dressed ladies with beautiful voices, and well-mannered husbands filled Weekly's room as Nastasya talked on of her life which had been lost forever. But Weekly, so full of the worry of how to get Nastasya away before she herself wanted to move, paid no attention, though Nastasya was sometimes very persistent and required Weekly to say, 'Did you now!', and 'Well I never!', at intervals. So again, one evening Weekly persuaded Nastasya.

'How's about a little walk Narsty?'

Nastasya immediately dressed herself and, with the white beret slapped on the side of her weatherbeaten face, she walked happily beside Weekly.

At the end of Claremont Street a brown dog came out from a garden, wagging his tail, he came up to them friendly and loving and lovable.

Nastasya laughed out loud.

'Oh Veekly, see his tail is like a question mark!' And then she said, 'Oh Veekly, only look what beautiful eyes he has,' Nastasya fondled the dog. 'See Veekly, his remarkable eyes, if you live a hundred years you could never see a human being with such eyes!'

Weekly looked at the dog and at Nastasya. No one was about in Claremont Street; it was as if the two elderly women and the dog were alone on a special spot, a corner of the earth set aside for moments of real understanding and discovery, one of those rare meeting places in the world where, quite unexpectedly, unfathomable depths of human feeling are exposed for just a few seconds, and it seems possible to come face to face with reality, and stand on the edge of the truth which can reveal forever the meaning of living.

When you knew the truth you died. Weekly was afraid to find out too much for this might bring about her own death. She was getting on, she knew this, but she wanted to live long enough to have her five acres.

'See Veekly', Nastasya was laughing over the dog. 'See

Veekly, if ever you see a man or a woman with eyes like this dog you would see a really remarkable person!'

How could Weekly tell Nastasya anything. They walked on in silence. When they were almost at the hospital Weekly wanted to explain to Nastasya where they were going. She tried to think of what to say.

Some children in the little park called out to the two old women, jeering at their strange old-fashioned clothes as they went slowly by, but Nastasya did not notice the children at all and she seemed quite unaware of Weekly's uneasiness.

'Hi Newspaper of Claremont Street!', the little boys called out, but Nastasya was laughing and, in her broken English, was saying, 'The air is so fresh today Veekly. I can forget now all my sadness, I can forget that I am sad. It will rain tonight. I can smell the rain is comink. Is good!'

Nastasya took in great gulps of air. When she spoke her voice was hoarse, 'I love this leetle park and the beeg trees!' Weekly thought about the life Nastasya would have in the hospital. She thought about Nastasya imprisoned with plastic sweet peas and roses and faded blankets and old pillows covered with waterproof material. She thought of the room which would be her confined world and the forlorn chair which would be her place forever and she tried to think of how she could explain to Nastasya it would be for her own good.

'Ich grenz an Gott!', Nastasya lifted her arms and seemed to be calling to the tree tops. 'My pronounciation of Cherman is very bad', she explained to Weekly. 'My Fraulein was such a dumpling I never paid any attention to her. Really, I suppose we despise the Germans. In our literature, our small characters, you know Veekly, the tutors and the poor ones are the Chermans, also they are unpleasant!'

They were almost through the park, just a short way from the hospital. Weekly tried to speak but Nastasya went on talking.

'Veekly here I am on the edge of God!' She talked on, 'I forget everything, it is terrible for me, but a learned chentle-

102

man, his name I cannot remember, but he was very clever, he
say,

'*A poet is a person to whom the visible world exists.*'

I don't suppose you could understand me Veekly.' Nastasya
paused on the path and looked at Weekly seriously. 'I tell
you this Veekly,' she said, 'not for you to understand the
clever man, but because once I was like the poet he described
and, because you bring me out to take air in the park, I begin
to feel alive once more. I see the grass and the trees and I can
smell the rain comink as I used to do.'

Nastasya stood in the middle of the path and looked at
Weekly and Weekly looked at Nastasya. She knew she could
not take her to the hospital. She was trapped. She was overcome by the unfairness of the world. She had once thought
that Nastasya had no one and that she, Weekly, had a street
full of people but, at this moment, she realised she, herself,
had no one. She would be forgotten within a few days of
leaving and no one would miss her. All she had was her land
and her solitude and this was to be taken over by Nastasya. If
only Nastasya could be quietly and kindly put out of the
way; her useless existence, which only survived by living on
Weekly, ended quickly and without fuss like the kittens
whose wailing was so easily and promptly extinguished. But
how could this be done? In the hospital Nastasya would have
to be visited. Weekly saw herself imprisoned there too on a
small wooden chair much too close to Nastasya's chair
endlessly listening to one complaint after another.

'Narsty, it's getting dark, we better turn back.' Weekly
took Nastasya's flabby arm. She had to force herself to make
the physical contact.

'You want me to stay with you?', Nastasya asked as if
she had sensed Weekly's intention.

'Why yes o' course I do', Weekly lied.

– 14 –

Nastasya was right about the rain. It came during the night pouring on the iron roof of the old house, a sustained hammering of rain gradually increasing in sound as it fell more heavily.

'Is like the wonderful last movement of the seventh symphony of Beethoven', Nastasya said in the dark. 'Only you Veekly cannot know what I mean, it is lost on someone like you! Oh,' she stretched herself in bed, 'is heavenly, the rain!'

But Weekly knew music which was like rain, she heard everything in the houses where she worked, often she polished with Mozart or Beethoven and talked down Bach. She tried to ignore Nastasya and listened to the rain in her own way as it came over the roof and rushed over the trembling gutters. The first rain on the dust and dry leaves brought a sharp fragrance up from the ground. It was like an anaesthetic, the smell of rain, almost too biting to breathe and yet it was impossible not to take deep breaths of the wonderful cool freshness after the intense heat and silence of the summer. Life seemed withdrawn during the summer, it was there of course, but hidden, the rain coming changed the season at once and brought the life out from its summer hiding place, back into the world.

Weekly thought about the five acres. Opposite her slope of land were upland paddocks half curtained by the big trees of the shallow ravine. During the hot weeks these paddocks, which were high and lifted up on the shoulders of the earth, were dry and brown. The rain would start them turning green over night. She listened to the rain happily. She thought about the cottage, if only she could be there at once. This last waiting was the hardest.

'Hope the roof doesn't leak', she muttered to herself. She thought about the creek at the bottom of her land. It had been dry all the summer. She tried to imagine how it would be flowing with water and how much water would flood the part Mr Rusk had described as flats. For the first time in her life she experienced real impatience. She wanted her land now. The coming of the rain and the smell of it in Claremont Street made her long for the greater fragrance she knew would be waiting for her up there.

The Newspaper of Claremont Street had no time to sit in the shop telling gossip and dwelling on the misfortunes of others. She was busy going to town to buy things. She bought a spade, rubber boots, some candles and groceries and polish and she began packing them into the old car. Last of all she bought a pear tree. It looked so wizened she wondered how it could ever grow. Carefully she wrapped it in wet newspapers and laid it like a thin baby along the back seat.

On the day Mr Rusk gave her the key, Weekly went to work with it pinned inside her dress. She felt it against her ribs all morning. She was glad of the perfumed, warm untidiness of Mrs Lacey's bedroom, and she tried to work quietly without too much excitement. The weeks had gone by and at last, after more rain and a great deal of patience, the money mountain was removed for ever from Weekly's sight. Her early morning picture, in the first light, was now of the cottage waiting alone for her to come. Every morning, before getting out of bed, she allowed herself a few moments to pause on the tiny threshold as if about to open the door.

No one was at home at the Laceys' so she was able to leave on time and instead of scrawling one of her notes, "Will spend more time on the bedroom floor next week. M.M.", instead of one of these little notes of promise and comfort there was nothing for Mrs Lacey except the clean house and a polite letter, written at home on cheap ruled paper the night before, explaining that owing to domestic reasons it would not be possible for her to come any more. And, instead of going on to the Chathams', she walked along Claremont Street dropping similar letters into all the letter boxes of the places where she had worked. Then she went on home to the room in the old house in Claremont Street. There she handed her key to the astonished landlady and she took her few clothes and bits of crockery and Nastasya and they drove together to Weekly's piece of land.

The same trees and fragrance and the cottage were all there as before. At once Nastasya discovered honeysuckle and roses, a fig tree and a hedge of rosemary, four little apple trees and an almond tree, all neglected and, for some reason, not seen by Weekly on her few visits there. While Nastasya talked, Weekly looked at all these things and saw they were waiting for her to continue with them what some other person had started a long time ago.

Weekly tried to move away from Nastasya. She felt she would die there that first day. A weakness seemed to spread all over her body and into her limbs as she opened the cottage door to look inside. She looked shyly, she was quite unlike herself, at the tiny rooms and then wandered about on the land looking at it and breathing the warm fragrance. The noise of the magpies poured into the stillness and she could hear the creek, in flood, running. She sank down on to the earth as if she would never get up from it again.

She counted over the treasures of the cottage. After having nothing she seemed now to have everything, a bed, a table, chairs and, in the kitchen, a wood stove and two toasting forks, a kettle and five flat irons. There was a painted cupboard and someone had made curtains of pale blue stuff, patterned all over with roses.

'See that red gum Veekly', Nastasya followed her about. 'That tree, Veekly, and some of the other beeg trees—', her voice went on and on. 'They must be three hondred years old at least!' Nastasya stood beside Weekly on the sunlit slope. 'When these trees were saplinks Veekly,' she said very seriously, 'do you realise that no white man knew that this country existed!'

Weekly knew she should clean out the cottage and Nastasya kept saying she was hungry but she wanted to rest on the earth and look about her, feeling the earth with her hands, and listening for some great wisdom to come to her from the quiet trees and the undergrowth. Somewhere out of sight, down at the edge of the creek, thousands of frogs were making a noise as if talking to each other.

'Veekly make me some coffee!' I am quite faint for some food. I like some coffee now Veekly, stronk and bleck!' Nastasya's voice interrupted. Better to clean the cottage and make Nastasya's special soup. Weekly made a great effort to get up. Tomorrow she would rest on the earth. She would look at the creek and discover its curves and its depths.

She began an unmerciful cleaning of the cottage.

'Awake my soul and with the sun . . .'

she sang as she cleaned. She took down the little curtains and washed them and spread them on the rosemary hedge to dry.

'Redeem thy misspent time that's past —
and live this day as if thy last,'

she polished the linoleum and washed out the cupboard and rubbed the tiny windows till they shone, singing all the time

'Awake my soul and with the sun —'

At about five o'clock the sun, before falling into the scrub, flooded the slope from the west and reddened the white bark of the trees. The sky deepened with the coming evening and Weekly put on the new rubber boots. She looked at Nastasya who was bent over greedily eating her food. The little kitchen seemed too full of Nastasya. She took the spade and the thin pear tree and still singing,

'Redeem thy misspent time that's past —
And live this day as if thy last —'

she went down to the bottom of her land.

There is something vulnerable about a person's back when bent unsuspectingly over food. The sight of Nastasya eating was a sad one and Weekly never wanted to hurt anyone if she could help it. Perhaps in some way she could atone for what she had done to Victor all those years ago by being kind to Nastasya. Besides she had been taught as a child never to take a person for granted. She tried not to think about Nastasya. She had looked forward for so long and so much to what was now hers. Just now she would forget Nastasya.

Bravely she walked all over the flats. She sank deep in the mud and the new boots were stuck all over with clay. With difficulty she pulled one foot out of the mud and then the other, exploring her land. She discovered that the creek came onto the property in two curves, one at each corner. There would be time to look at that in the morning. Choosing a place for the pear tree, she began to dig a hole. It was harder to dig in the clay than she thought and she had to pause to rest several times. Lovingly she looked at the little tree lying there waiting to grow. She could not really believe that it had any life. She tried to hurry with digging the hole. The tree must have a chance straight away.

'You don't understand, Veekly do you hear me? You don't understand the delicate operation of planting a tree', Nastasya called from the edge of the flats. 'Give me your boots and I show you. I know everything about planting a young tree!' If only Nastasya would give her peace to enjoy her land and let her be in peace to plant her tree.

'Give me your boots!', the voice went on and on spoiling the quiet evening. 'Give to me your boots!'

So Weekly stood barefoot in the soft mud and Nastasya,

with great difficulty, forced her larger feet into the boots.

'Now,' Nastasya said. 'See that bleck soil up on the slope where that beeg trees lies on the ground, not there Veekly, higher up.' Nastasya was more than a little impatient, Weekly looked up her land to where the fallen tree was.

'It did not fall Veekly,' Nastasya said, 'it was pushed there and a lot of bleck soil is under ziss tree, ziss soil you hev to fetch down here and put in this hole.'

So Weekly obediently went up and down with her bare feet fetching soil on the spade. She wanted to plant the tree and had looked forward to it. Nastasya's overbearing manner had become intolerable and she bitterly regretted not having taken her to the hospital. She found the burden of Nastasya far heavier in this place. These thoughts pushed aside any pleasure she would have had planting the tree.

'Hurry Veekly! My beck is breaking!' Nastasya was bending over holding the tree in the hole, the mud was half way up the new boots as she had sunk into the clay. 'Scatter the fine bleck soil round the roots.' Nastasya ordered. She shook the tree so that the soil fell closely around the fine roots. Again and again Nastasya shook the tree and Weekly scattered in more soft dark soil.

'And now,' Nastasya said straightening her back a little, 'you must tread round and round the tree. I cannot as I am stuck, as you see!', and she laughed.

So Weekly firmed the soil, treading gently round and round the tree, passing close to the tree and to Nastasya. She had to step between them.

For the first time in her life the Newspaper of Claremont Street was dancing. Stepping round and round the little tree she was like a bride dancing. She imagined a veil of lacy white blossom falling all around her. Round and round the tree, dancing, firming the softly yielding earth with her bare feet. And from the little foil label, blowing in the restlessness of the evening, came a fragile music for the pear tree dance.

'Hurry Veekly!, it is gettink colder and the dark iss coming. Enough now!', Nastasya ordered, but Weekly went

109

on dancing. She forgot Nastasya for a moment. There was a smoothness and ease about her bare feet on the soft, black soil and the little tree seemed comfortable at last. Weekly looked at its tiny twig-like trunk, perhaps it was not dead after all. It looked glossy and stood bravely there in the dusk. She began to walk slowly up her land still dancing, it seemed, only more slowly; she heard the tiny label, it was like strange faint music.

'Veekly! help me!' Nastasya's voice broke into the dream dance. Nastasya was stuck fast in the wet clay, the new boots were now quite covered by the mud and Nastasya was unable to pull her large swollen feet out of them.

'Veekly you have to get me out from here! It's so cold now and tonight it will freeze!' Nastasya's voice rose to a pathetic scream as she called after Weekly. 'Veekly!', the voice followed Weekly up the slope.

'Veekly help me! You cannot leave me. Tonight it will freeze. It is so lonely here no one can hear me except you. Help me!'

Yes, Nastasya was probably right. She usually was about the weather and the names of trees and plants and everything. It would be freezing tonight. Fortunately there was some wood chopped ready for the stove. As she pulled the scraps of blue curtain from the hedge of rosemary before going into her cottage, Weekly could feel the chill stiffness of the coming frost already in the damp material.

She was not now able to hear Nastasya's voice. The distance was a little too great. In the fast falling dusk she was just able to see her down there. She could make out a grey figure alone in the cold grey evening, and it looked as if Nastasya was dancing the pear tree dance.

110

-15-

It had become the fashion to buy land. All kinds of people were searching for week-end country properties, farmlets they called them. The price òf land rose steadily. The township became more desolate as more and more country people, unable to make a living, moved to the city to find work and to live in the new housing estates.

Poor quality fruit was unsaleable and pear trees were bulldozed into the ground. Almond orchards were ruined by the goats which were allowed to roam between the trees. Some houses and sheds were soon in a decrepit and neglected state.

People coming out to improve property, even if only at week-ends, was a good thing and the postmistress·of White Gum crossing welcomed the newcomers. The post office was a small fenced-off part of the general store. With great foresight the postmistress stocked up with handles for mattocks and axes, green netting for hats, and she had wheat for the kind of poultry townspeople are foolish enough to keep as pets. In her shed, she had fencing wire and paint and she began ordering greater supplies of foodstuffs in preparation for the increasing week-end population.

One of the visitors from the city was a fair-haired, stocky man, middle aged and with a quiet disposition. He came often to look and, after a time, he bought a piece of land. He liked to think of himself as the squire of the scattered township which was near his property. He dressed himself in new country clothes and drank beer with the local inhabitants on Saturday evenings. He strode about his paddocks inspecting fence posts and he did a little burning off at the right times. At night he sat studying pamphlets on soil analysis, trickle irrigation and fruit fly. He wrote long letters to many firms asking about trees and machinery and equipment. He was a handsome man, though no longer young, and many people in the little town thought it was a shame he was not married. Such a man could make some woman happy and secure for life. It was a great pity he had no family.

'It's a waste of a good man', the woman at the post office said to him one day. She was in a talkative mood.

'I suppose you realise you paid too much for that place you bought,' she said, 'would have bought it myself but I said to myself that land at that price is sheer robbery.' She paused and put a stamp on an envelope. 'You'll have trouble with all that swamp on your block, the river flats, know where I mean?' She waited a moment and went on, 'You could go up the road and see what the Dutchman's done at his place. Where the clay pits are, you'll know the place when you see it. You never saw such a mess. Seems to me all your place is good for is the same as what they're doing there. Why don't you toddle up there and have a mosey round?'

He paid for his stamp, he agreed it was a pity he had no wife and he thanked her for her helpful talk about his land. In spite of the problems of the poor land, he continued to enjoy his new life and, as soon as he could, he moved out to live in the country instead of just going there at week-ends.

One afternoon he dressed himself with great care and set out to call on his neighbour on the next property. He had

112

heard, on another occasion from the postmistress, that a lady lived there quite alone.

With a springing step he crossed his dried-up paddocks and followed the rubbish-filled creek bed for a few hundred yards. Then he picked and pushed his way through the overgrown bush which bordered on his own neat place. He came to a little clearing some way up the slope. There was a tiny weatherboard cottage with two crazily painted notices,

Pears For Sale

and,

Firewood Cheap

by the door. At first he thought no one was there – it was so still.

'Anyone at home?', he called. 'Anyone at home?', he called again. He walked round the house and came upon an old woman bending down tying up sticks into little bundles.

'Good afternoon madam', he said. She straightened up and, shading her eyes with one hand, she peered at him.

'Aw my Gawd!', she said, suddenly out of breath. 'I'll have to set down a minute yo've give me a shock.' He helped her to the broken steps of the verandah.

Weekly had to breathe hard for a moment.

'Funny old day', she said to him, cackling to hide her silliness. 'Funny old day with all this cloud and no rain. But o' course,' she added, 'the sun's shining up there in the sky on the other side of the cloud. Learned us that at school didn't they.'

'Yes. Yes they did', he agreed. He was wondering whether he should have come.

'It's yor voice,' she said, 'yor voice, it reminded me of someone', she thought she ought to explain her confusion. 'For a minute there yo' had me bothered.' She sank into her own thoughts. It was so long since she had heard that over refined way of speaking which did not completely conceal its origin.

'I've bought the property adjoining yours', he explained

113

gently.

'Have you now, that's very nice', she said, composing herself and remembering her manners, 'how about I make you some tea?', she asked. 'Come in and set down.' He helped her up on to the verandah. He had not expected the lady living alone on the next property to be so elderly, but there was something he liked about her and he supposed age did not matter in the nature of the proposal he had to make.

'Well, perhaps, yes tea would be very acceptable', he realised how much he needed some after his difficult walk.

They drank their tea together, with appreciation. Weekly, used to being alone always, tried to drink hers more quietly than she usually did. It was quite a strain being well mannered. The visitor was a mystery too; he did not resemble Victor at all in looks and, of course, a great many people spoke like that, even the tone of the voice, which was so familiar, could belong to many people.

He seemed excited about his idea. He described the clay and the brick-making. His tea cup rattled on the saucer so Weekly took it from him. She listened attentively, fascinated more by the sound of the voice than by the idea which seemed to involve using part of her land, and part of his, for something she could never want. They walked together slowly down the fragrant slope to the river flats. As the sun fell into the scrub on the other side of the valley the last rays reddened the white bark of Weekly's ghost gums. The evening was coming quickly.

'This would be the area involved', he waved his arm towards the flats. I have a similar patch adjoining.' They walked together along the edge of the hard dry clay.

'In winter,' he said, 'this clay is very wet and deep and sticky. It's too soft for anything in winter.'

'Yerse,' Weekly said. 'I know.'

'This clay makes special bricks, but,' he sighed, 'even the best bricks crumble to dust in the end,' he sighed again. 'Nothing lasts for ever'.

They walked on slowly. For a while neither of them spoke.

114

'I see you are trying to grow some fruit', he said with reverence, pausing beside a tree.

'Yerse', Weekly said. 'That's my pear tree. It takes a while for pear trees to grow. I'm hopin' to get some fruit nex' year. Plant pears for yor heirs! So they say.'

Next to the pear tree was a curious earth-covered mound about the size of a man bent double. It was fenced roughly with pieces of old pipe and bits of wood and bark, some tin cans had been hammered flat and stuck into the clay.

'It's quite an art piece,' he said.

'Yerse,' Weekly agreed. 'I should like this left as it is too,' she said, 'I suppose if you, if we, have the clay pit, I should be very much obliged if me bit of fence could be left undisturbed. In a coupla hundred years there should be a interesting fossil here. In the interests of science, you see.'

'Yes,' he said, 'in the interests of science of course. We should, if you agree, and you must think about it, we should get a lot of clay out of here,' he said, 'a lot of clay,' he was quiet and thoughtful as if calculating clay.

They began to walk up the slope together. The thirty-four rows of herring-bone stitch on Weekly's skirts looked purple and expensive in the dusk.

The moon was rising behind the tall gum trees. The persistent tremulous movement of the long leaves in front of the shining moon made it look as if little candle flames were flickering all around the outside edges of it.

'Oh just look at that wonderful moon', he said.

'Yerse,' Weekly said, 'er fairly races up the sky of a night. Er looks a bit undecided,' she said. She was out of breath.

'Well I suppose I better be going home', he said at the door of the cottage. Weekly thought for a moment that perhaps she should invite him indoors. Unable to make up her mind, she let the thought go.

She watched him disappear into the night. Sooner or later they would have to tell each other their names as it was the usual thing to do. She supposed that he would come back, though she thought to herself that she would not mind at all if he did not. As for the name, she was not sure that she wanted to know what it was.